WARRIOR FORBIDDEN

SAMANTHA CHARLTON

Warrior Forbidden, by Samantha Charlton

Published by Winter Mist Press

ISBN: 978-1-7385901-6-2 (paperback)

Edited by Tim Burton
Cover images generated by Midjourney
Cover design by Winter Mist Press

Visit Sam's website: www.samanthacharltonauthor.com

Giving in to temptation could destroy them both. In another galaxy, another time, a priestess and her security chief must protect an ancient temple against rebels—while fighting the forbidden fire that smolders between them.

Ava's life has been dedicated to protecting the sacred flame upon a dying planet. Years ago, she swore a life of chastity and obedience to honor the Gods, yet now everything she cares about is under threat.

A group of religious extremists is targeting her and the temple she guards. **Her order needs help, but that means letting *men* set foot in her temple— something that hasn't happened in a thousand years.**

Jax commands a corps of elite soldiers. The Guardians of the Flame have been tasked to guard the Sisters of Awe, to train them in self-defense—and to deal with the insurgents who will stop at nothing to create chaos.

When Jax and Ava meet, a battle of wills begins. She wants as little interference in the daily life of her temple as possible, while he's determined to make some big changes to ensure her safety.

Sparks fly—but what starts off as animosity between Ava and the stubborn captain, soon becomes something else entirely.

Something forbidden to them both.

*Love is love, even if it is illicit; like light remains light
even in the darkness.*
—Munia Khan

In another time …
In another galaxy …

1. A MARKED WOMAN

CROUCHED ON THE landing platform, the shuttle resembled the slain carcass of some monstrous grey-plated beetle. But unfortunately, it wasn't an insect, and it wasn't dead either. And soon, it would spew a host of unwelcome visitors.

Ava approached it warily, her stride slowing as she drew near. A warm wind tugged at her, causing the crimson cloak she wore to billow. The whirr of rubber wheels on stone behind Ava warned that DD-J3 was following at her heels. Her utility-droid was equipped with protocol capabilities and could communicate in many galactic languages. These warriors would likely speak Rith, the common language throughout the sector, yet she'd brought Dee Dee with her anyway.

Dragging in a deep breath, Ava focused on keeping her heart-rate steady, her temper leashed. She'd been dreading this moment—when the soldiers who'd been recruited to form the elite guard would arrive.

For the first time in over three centuries, *males* would set foot on this planet.

Ava's mouth thinned, her anger simmering. Such strong emotion was frowned upon in her order; the High Priestess especially was to remain sanguine at all times.

It was impossible to stay calm though.

These warriors were here to protect her and her sisters, but Pillarus One and this sacred temple would be defiled by their presence. This was wrong—but the choice wasn't hers, for the Wise Ones had authorized it.

Glancing left, Ava's gaze traveled to the tower that had been carved, like the temple itself, out of the mountain behind her. It thrust skyward like a blunted blade, stained dark-blood-red in the perpetual dusk of the twilight zone. This thin boundary between Pillarus One's eternal day and endless night was the only habitable area upon the planet, as it orbited a dying red dwarf sun. Tidally locked to the sun, Pillarus One had the same rotational period as its orbit around its sun. There were no seasons here—just a dark side that was unhospitable and freezing, and a light side hot enough to boil water. There had once been oceans on Pillarus One, yet they'd boiled away on the light side and had long since frozen on the dark side.

Ava's gaze narrowed as she viewed the Tower of Flame, where the Wise Ones resided. No, she wouldn't question their will—no one did—but that didn't mean she was happy about this.

The hiss of hydraulics drew her attention away from the tower and back to the shuttle.

The dying whine of its engines joined the whistling of the wind. And then, as Ava looked on, the hatch on its side opened and its ramp lowered to the landing platform.

Halting a few yards back, Ava folded her arms across her chest and waited. Meanwhile, Dee Dee rattled to a halt next to her, lights blinking on its domed head. Apart from her utility-droid, she was alone here. She had deliberately not brought any of her sisters with her, even Skylar, her Second. These marines were unwelcome— they wouldn't be met by a party of curious, and excited, priestesses.

Indeed, Ava intended to keep the Sisters of Awe and the Guardians of the Flame as separate as possible. Her sisters couldn't be distracted from their duties.

A tall, broad-shouldered figure appeared in the gangway then. And despite her best efforts to maintain her serenity, Ava's heart kicked hard against her ribs.

She hadn't seen a man—or indeed any male, human or otherwise—since taking her vows fifteen years earlier.

Clad in black-and-crimson-plated armor, a scarlet cloak rippling from broad shoulders, the soldier was big—bigger than most human males. He wore a red-crested, visored helmet that masked the top half of his face. Gleaming obsidian bracers protected his forearms, and heavy greaves covered muscular calves.

The newcomer paused in the gangway for a moment, his visored gaze sweeping his surroundings. An instant later, he saw Ava and stilled.

His calm was almost predatory, and Ava's heart bucked hard once more.

Gods, who had the clan-lords sent to protect her?

And then, a second later, the warrior was marching down the ramp, armor creaking, and heading straight toward Ava. He halted just two yards distant, that eerie visored gaze gleaming dark red in the light of the red dwarf glowing above. Her attention shifted to the lower half of his face: a lantern jaw, and the harsh slash of a mouth that looked as if it rarely curved into a smile.

Ava swallowed. She supposed she should greet him, yet her tongue suddenly felt as if it were stuck to the roof of her mouth.

Dammit, she'd told herself she wouldn't let any of these newcomers intimidate her, and here she was, rendered speechless.

"Greetings," Dee Dee spoke up then, its high-pitched voice carrying across the landing platform. "Welcome to Pillarus One and the Temple of the Gods."

The soldier nodded. He then reached up and removed his helmet.

Ava's breathing caught. If she had thought the man was intimidating with the helmet on, he was terrifying without it. His face was strong-featured and so stern it appeared carven of stone. He had thick black hair with a pronounced widow's peak, and a heavy brow and piercing black eyes beneath it.

And that obsidian gaze pinned her to the ground.

"I am Jax Mir-Lelith," he rumbled. "Captain of the Guardians of the Flame."

He fell silent then, waiting for Ava to speak.

"You stand before Ava Mir-Brennan, High Priestess of the Sisters of Awe," she eventually replied, cursing the hoarseness in her voice.

The captain nodded once more. It was a sign of respect, yet his expression didn't change. It was as forbidding as earlier.

"Welcome," she said after another awkward pause before inwardly kicking herself. Dee Dee had already welcomed the man; she didn't need to do it again. Ava then glanced behind him at the empty gangway. "Have you brought a security team with you?"

Captain Jax nodded. "I have twenty warriors with me … and another fifty onboard a light battlecruiser orbiting this planet … are our lodgings prepared?"

Irritation speared Ava. Did he think she was his housekeeper? Lucky for him, she wasn't about to ignore the orders of the Wise Ones—or the urgent requests of the sector's clan rulers.

"Yes," she replied, her tone clipped now. "You and your team will be living in barracks outside the temple." She gestured to the low-slung building, made of the same fawn-colored stone as the temple itself, sitting at the base of the rocky outcrop from which it reared.

However, when she glanced back at the captain, his black brows had knitted together into a frown. "I'd prefer our lodgings to be *inside* the temple," he said, his deep voice reverberating across the landing platform.

Ava scowled back.

That wasn't going to happen. "And *I'd* prefer you resided outside."

Captain Jax folded his muscular arms across his armored chest and looked down his straight nose at her. Ava was a tall, well-built woman. However, to hold that disconcerting inky gaze, she had to crane her neck.

"For your safety, my chamber must be within easy reach of yours, My Lady," he replied.

Ava's heart started pounding. *What?* "That's not necessary."

His gaze didn't waver from hers. It was as if he hoped to stare her into submission. "It is," he replied. "You must realize that your life is in danger."

Ava's already racing heart kicked up another notch. "That's a bit of an exaggeration, isn't it?" she said, glad that her voice didn't betray how annoyed she was becoming now. "*The Creed of Truth* isn't after me personally."

"They're dedicated to bringing this temple, and everything it stands for, down … to establishing a new order where they rule this sector, and only one God is revered." His jaw tightened just a fraction, betraying his own irritation. "*You* are the figurehead of everything they want to destroy. I'm not trying to scare you, High Priestess, but you're a marked woman."

A sickly sensation washed over Ava.

She knew that *The Creed of Truth*—the group of religious extremists loyal to Wis, the Seer of Truth—had grown in strength over the past years. Initially, they'd gained influence on backwater worlds, yet in the past months, they'd actively targeted prominent temples dedicated to other Galactic Gods throughout the Rith Sector.

The Sisters of Awe lived apart from others. None of the clans had intruded upon the order's reclusion in centuries. However, the Temple of the Gods wasn't just sacred to those who protected it, but to everyone in the sector who held the Gods dear. An attack on the temple would send shockwaves throughout the galaxy and risk widespread panic and anarchy. As such, the clan leaders had offered their protection—and to Ava's shock, the Wise Ones agreed.

Of course, she'd swallowed their orders—but having Captain Jax and his soldiers residing inside the temple, letting them sleep near her and her sisters, was taking things too far.

"Surely, you can put security measures in place *around* the temple instead?" she said after a lengthy pause. However, her tone wasn't so certain now. In truth, the captain's words had rattled her. She'd only just met him, but Ava sensed he wasn't a man to make careless comments.

Her skin prickled then. Maybe she *was* in danger.

"We shall be doing a thorough audit of your security," he assured her, his expression never changing. "But that's in addition to ensuring your personal safety."

Ava stared back at him, a stone settling in the pit of her stomach.

Captain Jax wouldn't budge. He was as inflexible as Lazda Steel. "It is the will of all the clan leaders that I and my warriors guard you with our lives," he said after a lengthy pause. "We are all veterans. I led the Mir-Lelith special forces until I volunteered for this position." He bowed his head then, in another sign of reverence. "And I'm honored to defend you."

Ava's jaw snapped closed.

His deference got on her nerves. It was fake, since he'd made it clear he wouldn't be using the barracks she'd had built for the Guardians of the Flame. He might have been 'honored', but not enough to heed her wishes.

He didn't seem to care that there might not be any space inside the temple for him and his team. Unfortunately, there was though. Once, this temple had been *full* of priestesses dedicated to watching over the sacred flame and honoring the Gods. But these days, acolytes were far fewer.

"Very well," she said, her tone clipped. "If your people are ready to disembark, my droid will show you all inside."

"That is appreciated, My Lady," he replied, his face as inscrutable as a cyborg's. "I'm happy for your droid to assist my team." He paused then, his gaze drilling into her. "However, I'd prefer *you* to show me around the temple personally."

2. GUARDING THE FLAME

HE'D PISSED HER off; that much was clear.

The woman's thinly veiled hostility surprised him. Weren't the Sisters of Awe supposed to be serene?

There wasn't any point in getting angry at him either. Her order had permitted this, after all. They'd agreed to aid from the three most powerful clans in the sector—the Mir-Brennans, the Mir-Ferrins, and the Mir Leliths—and the clan leaders had put forward their best to form this specialist security force.

But if Jax had expected the High Priestess to show some gratitude, he was out of luck.

Her nostrils flared as she stared up at him, and her dark-grey eyes narrowed. He was impressed that she held his gaze so fiercely. Most people found him intimidating.

Jax wasn't sure what he'd been expecting the High Priestess of the Sisters of Awe to be like—but Ava Mir-Lelith wasn't it.

She was younger than he'd imagined, for one. He'd known she was new to this position, for her predecessor had died suddenly around six months earlier. Nonetheless, she looked to be in her early thirties at most. The human female was tall and strong, and the high-necked red tunic she wore couldn't conceal an impressive bust. She had clear skin and pale-blonde hair, cut so it framed her face.

She was attractive, if in a haughty, cold way. Or she would have been if she wasn't scowling at him.

Jax let his request that *she* be the one to show him around hang in the air between them. He could see she was struggling—that she wanted to refuse him. But she stopped herself.

It cost her though, the muscles in her jaw flexing.

Silence swelled between them, and Jax waited. He was patient, and he liked to have the upper hand in situations. It was important to establish control from the outset or this woman would cause him problems. A cool wind buffeted them, and a dust devil twirled across the platform behind the High Priestess.

Eventually, the woman huffed a sharp, irritated sigh. "Very well." She then shifted her attention to the droid squatting next to her. "Dee Dee, take the soldiers to accommodation zones D and E."

Lights blinked on the droid's domed head. "Yes, Mistress."

Jax favored her with a nod of thanks in reply before tapping his chunky wrist-comm. "First Officer Vander," he said tersely. "You and the others can disembark now and unload the equipment. There's a utility-droid waiting to take you to our lodgings inside the temple."

"Copy, Captain," a deep male voice replied.

Jax met the High Priestess's gaze once more before gesturing toward the path that led up from the landing platform to the entrance of the temple. "After you, My Lady."

Her nostrils flared once more, and then she swiveled on her heel and stalked off, stiff-backed and head held high.

Jax followed.

And as he walked, he surveyed his surroundings.

Ever since he'd disembarked from the shuttle, Lady Ava had held his attention. However, as their light cruiser, which now orbited Pillarus One, approached the planet earlier, he'd viewed it with interest.

Like most citizens of the Rith Sector, he'd learned about this reclusive order, dedicated to worshipping the Galactic Gods, as a child. He'd also heard this planet was dying, and it seemed the rumors were true.

Stained red by the red dwarf sun, and orbited by three silver moons, Pillarus One appeared to be reaching the end of its time as a habitable planet. Tidally locked to its sun, it now only had a terminator—a thin ring of land—where sentient beings could exist. As they'd flown in, Jax had seen just how narrow twilight eternity was. No more than forty klicks between the scorching side that faced the sun, and the dark side of the planet that appeared to be partially covered in ice.

The Sisters of Awe had chosen Pillarus One for a reason. A long time ago, those who'd settled here had sought seclusion so that they could honor the Gods without distraction. They'd moved from their original planet, once it became uninhabitable, and sent out priests and priestesses to set up temples to the various Gods throughout the galaxy. Word had spread, yet the heart of the order, and the ancient beings that presided over it—was on Pillarus One.

This world, the first of five similarly-named planets in this solar system—and the only one where life existed—sat on the outer fringes of Mir-Lelith territory, far from other habitable planets or the busy trade routes that crisscrossed the sector.

But now that he'd landed, Jax had to admit that the place possessed a certain stark beauty. A sculpted, mountainous landscape stretched out around him in all directions. The dark-red and deeply shadowed hills and crags around the temple faded to deep pink at the horizon. Above it all, looming huge in the dark sky, hung the planet's nearest moon, Janessa. Named after a mythical handmaid to the Gods, its heavily pockmarked silvery surface stood out in detail against the dark sky.

The path rose sharply as they made their way up through razor-sharp rocks to where the temple reared up. The Temple to the Gods looked as if it had been carved out of the rock it sat upon. Its main structure was hive-shaped with a ring of narrow towers around it that tapered off into delicate spires, while at the top of the mountain, a lonely tower, much larger than all the rest, pierced the sky.

Jax's brow furrowed, even as the hair on the back of his arms prickled. The Tower of Flame—where the Wise Ones, the most enigmatic beings in this sector—resided.

Here he was, the first male in centuries to set foot inside the temple itself.

Jax and his team weren't just here to ensure the High Priestess and her sisters weren't harmed—but to ensure *The Creed of Truth* never got near that tower. This temple and the Wise Ones that had dwelt within the Tower of Flame for millennia could not come to any harm. This was the spiritual center for billions of souls within the sector.

They entered the temple through a wide carven arch, walking into a vast, echoey entrance hall with a dome-vaulted ceiling. The stone in here was a light fawn, although the ruddy light filtering in through the open doorway still managed to wash the interior with its red stain.

Their boots whispered on smooth pavers as they walked between rows of thick, imposing columns.

"This is the atrium," the High Priestess said, speaking for the first time since they'd left the landing platform. She motioned then to a large staircase that rose from the far end. A service elevator stood to one side of it. "The accommodation zones, as well as my solar, the conservatory, and the library, are located upstairs."

Jax met her eye. "And the chapel itself?" He was interested in seeing every corner of this place, but first, he wanted to see the fabled Flame Chapel—a place only these priestesses had been allowed access to for centuries.

And as their gazes held, Jax noted how Ava Mir-Brennan's jaw tightened once more.

Even now, she was inwardly railing at this.

Once again, Jax waited for her to answer. It was his way. He knew what power there was in letting others fill a silence. This woman wasn't in charge here any longer—*he* was.

The High Priestess drew in a slow, deep breath, her shoulders squaring. "All right," she said stiffly. "This way."

Without another word, she turned her back on Jax and strode toward an archway that led off to the left.

He followed her through a cool corridor, lined with glow-lamps. Moments later, they stepped out into a wide space. At least four times the size of the cavernous atrium, the Flame Chapel was a sight indeed.

The first thing that struck Jax was the atmosphere in here. The air held a charge that made his pulse quicken in response. The next thing he noticed was that nothing inside the chapel was a straight line: the walls, the ceiling, even the altar itself—where a large red-gold flame burned upon a brazier—were all gently curved. The ceiling was domed and painted in intricate murals depicting the Gods, while a circular hole at its apex let in the murky crimson-stained light.

Jax's breathing grew shallow, and he fought the overwhelming urge to sink to his knees in reverence. His mother had brought him up to honor the Gods, and his devotion was one reason he'd been chosen for this position.

The Eight formed a silent watch over the sacred flame. Each of the High Gods was carved out of what looked like pale Morvinian marble. Few stones glowed like that in firelight.

Jax's gaze slid over Raul, the Destroyer; Jidea, Goddess of Fortune; Miradia, Goddess of Fertility; the twin sisters—Fara, Lady of Light, and Nain, Lady of Darkness; Aura, Goddess of Prosperity; and Syr, God of Mercy.

However, his gaze lingered on this last statue—Wis, the Seer of Truth. The God's face had been sculpted into an expression of serenity and kindness. The robed figure stood tall and proud, his hands raised in a gesture of welcome and acceptance.

The irony wasn't lost on Jax.

Of all the Galactic Gods, Wis had always been the one that pacifists had been drawn to. And yet, somehow, a faction had emerged over the past years, a group of acolytes who believed that Wis was the one, the *only*, God.

The Creed believed that any who worshipped the others were heretics—and that meant that their enemies were numerous. They'd publicly condemned the leaders of the Mir-Brennan, Mir-Ferrin, and Mir-Lelith clans on the Shadownet for their 'hubris'. According to *The Creed*, the clan leaders had raised themselves too high, acting as if they were Gods themselves. And of course, this temple, with its sacred flame and host of priestesses dedicated to serving the Eight, as well as the numerous lesser Gods, was an offense to the extremists.

Jax's attention shifted then, from Wis to the two priestesses, in flesh and blood, who stood watch over the sacred flame. His breathing grew shallower still at the sight of the fire that burned in a wide metal bowl behind the sisters.

Swallowing, Jax did yield to the sacredness of this place. He lowered himself to the ground then, on one knee. Head bowed, he whispered a prayer, honoring each of the Eight in turn.

He couldn't stand before the Flame of the Gods—a fire that had burned for millennia—and not show respect.

The Flame of the Gods kept the connection between the heavens and the earth united. It was said that if it ever went out, the Gods would turn their backs on mortals and the universe would dissolve into chaos. As such, the clan leaders were heavily invested in keeping it safe.

There was a part of Jax, the cynical, practical part, that doubted this. All the same, he was awed by the sight of the tender golden flames flickering before him.

Rising to his feet, his attention returned to the two stern-faced human females who stood before the altar, gazes fixed ahead, hands clasped in front of them. Jax's gaze slid over the Sisters, taking in the rigid stance of their red-robed forms and the way they were both doing their best *not* to stare at him.

Impressive.

That took a lot of self-control for, like their High Priestess, these two would be unnerved by his presence here.

Jax continued to observe them. Both priestesses were young, under twenty-five, and slender. And they didn't appear to be armed. His gaze narrowed. What was the point of guarding the Flame of the Gods, if they had no way of defending it against intruders?

He glanced over at the High Priestess to see that she was watching him, her eyebrows knitted together. She didn't like how closely he was taking note of his surroundings, but he didn't care.

It was his job.

He met her gaze squarely. "Where are the priestess's weapons?" he asked, his voice echoing in the stillness.

A muscle feathered in the High Priestess's jaw. "No weapons are allowed in here." Her gaze strayed then to the grip of the laser-blade he carried at his right hip, and the laser-pistol strapped to his left thigh, silent disapproval emanating from her.

Jax stared back, challenging her, before allowing his mouth to curve into the barest hint of a smile. "That, My Lady, will have to change."

3. SOME LINES WON'T BE CROSSED

HEAT ROLLED OVER Ava, and she started to sweat.
Enough.

It was bad enough this arrogant, armed *male* had stridden into their hallowed temple and surveyed the interior as if he owned it—but now he was talking about changing rules that had stood for the past thousand years. The Sisters of Awe weren't pacifists, yet weapons were forbidden inside the Flame Chapel. This space was sacred.

"To bear weapons inside this space is a direct challenge to the Gods," she said finally, trying her best to keep her anger from showing in her voice. "This is a place of worship … and of peace. You have given offense."

The captain's gaze, as black as obsidian, bored into her. "I showed the Eight the proper respect," he replied, reminding her that he'd knelt and offered prayers upon entering the chapel. "But the old ways are going to change. Those guarding the flame need to be armed … otherwise, they're useless."

"The Flame Watch is *symbolic*," Ava replied. "We tend it rather than protect it, showing the Gods the proper respect … that isn't useless. Devotion *is* power."

He snorted. "And after *The Creed of Truth* kills you, the chapel will be where they strike next."

Captain Jax's words caused Luna, one of the priestesses standing before the altar, to stifle a gasp.

Ava cut the younger woman a stern look. *Hold fast.* Those taking the Watch of the Flame had to remain unmoved during their shift. They weren't to speak, weren't to move. Luna wasn't one to break the rules, but the captain's words had clearly shocked her.

Likewise, next to her, Maya's thin face had paled. The second of the priestesses guarding the flame looked as if she might faint.

"These aren't empty threats, My Lady," Captain Jax went on, his deep voice rumbling through the temple like thunder. "*The Creed of Truth* has publicly vowed to destroy this place and everything it stands for." His dark eyebrows drew together as he continued to stare her down. "The clan leaders have taken this declaration seriously … and so should you."

Ava swallowed, even as another wave of prickling heat washed over her.

It was bad enough that from the moment he'd stepped off his shuttle, this man had aggressively challenged her—but to do it in front of her sisters was humiliating indeed.

She wanted to grab the bastard by the arm and drag him away before letting her fury loose on him. However, to lose her temper, especially in this sacred place, would be sacrilege. "We shall discuss this later," she replied, her voice clipped.

"There's nothing to discuss, My Lady." His tone was obstinate, his gaze inflexible. "You might be against it, but I must ensure the safety of this temple any way I can. That means that your priestesses *will* carry weapons" His attention shifted from her then, traveling up to the domed roof above, and the circular hole at its apex. "Does that remain open at all times?"

"No," Ava replied, barely able to speak as rage pounded through her. "There's a Lazda Steel shutter … for emergency use only."

"Good," he grunted. "Although it should be closed at all times … it's a security risk."

Red veiled Ava's vision as her temper came dangerously close to snapping. Gods, she was never this volatile. However, Captain Jax Mir-Lelith really had taken things too far. "That can't happen." She bit out the words. "This chapel requires direct access to the sky … the link between the sacred flame and heavens is vital."

"It's also an open invitation for a spy-drone or assassins," he shot back, irritation creeping into his voice for the first time. "Like it or not, My Lady, you have to accept that *The Creed* is on its way."

Ava stared back at him. Her belly tightened then at his warning. She'd kept informed about the worsening situation with the extremists, yet this man's arrival made everything seem more real.

Suddenly, it felt as if *The Creed* were breathing down the back of her neck.

All the same, she wasn't going to let him use it to bully her.

"Be that as it may, I will not have your security measures compromising our worship," she answered stiffly. "You do what you must to ensure we're all kept safe … but some lines won't be crossed."

Their gazes locked, the seconds ticking by. Ava was aware that both Luna and Maya were watching her now—even without glancing their way, she could feel the weight of their stares.

She'd reprimand them both later for letting themselves be distracted from their watch, but for the moment, Ava's attention didn't shift from Captain Jax's stone-hewn face.

He'd pushed her far enough, dominating this sacred space as if it belonged to him. She wouldn't have him dictate to her, and she'd fight him with everything she had, if he continued to push.

The wind had gotten up. It buffeted against the thick stone walls of the temple, howling under the eaves, and clawing at the windows.

Standing in his bedchamber, Jax stared out at the twilight.

He kept expecting night to fall, and yet the sky never changed. That would take some getting used to, as would many things here.

Jax's mouth thinned. His arrival hadn't gone as smoothly as he'd hoped.

The High Priestess, whose cooperation he depended upon, was uptight and inflexible. She knew the danger the order was in yet seemed unwilling to make the necessary changes.

Luckily, he wasn't a man to give up at the first hurdle. And he wasn't about to let Ava Mir-Brennan call the shots.

The woman had more changes coming, and she wouldn't like any of them.

Turning from the window, Jax let his gaze travel over the chamber he'd been given. It was austere and sparsely furnished, with exposed stone walls. All the same, his new lodgings were far bigger and more comfortable than his berth back on *The Star-Hawk*, the cruiser that now orbited Pillarus One.

"Captain," a tinny voice intruded then. "Would you care for refreshments?"

Jax's gaze came to rest upon a squat utility-droid. It was similar to the one that had waited with the High Priestess on the landing platform earlier, an older model than the Mir-Lelith clan-lord used. However, that was to be expected, for the Sisters of Awe lived simply in their remote corner of the sector.

Jax was about to dismiss the offer when he hesitated. He didn't usually drink on the job, but after locking horns with the High Priestess, he needed something to mellow himself before he faced the woman again. He was to join her and the others in the dining hall within the hour. "Do you have any Morith whisky?" he asked hopefully.

"Yes, Sir," the droid chirped. "The replicator has been provided for your comfort. Would you like something to eat as well?"

"No." Frankly, Jax was surprised they were serving him whisky, for he knew the Sisters of Awe abstained from alcohol, smoking clove, or using any other mind-altering substances. But it seemed they'd made an exception for him.

"Do you require ice, Sir?"

"No."

The utility-droid rolled over toward a gleaming silver cube attached to the wall. Meanwhile, Jax turned back to the window.

The wind was starting to punch at the glass now, making it tremble under the force. From here, he had a view down the winding path he'd climbed earlier, to the landing platform, where his shuttle still sat.

"Is it often windy here?" he asked, glancing over his shoulder at where the droid's metal claw had just grasped around a tumbler of amber-hued liquid. It then turned and trundled toward him.

"Pillarus One has an extremely windy climate," the droid replied. "Hurricanes, dust-storms, and tornadoes are frequent."

Jax frowned. Stabbing a finger at his wrist-comm, he then spoke into it. "First Officer Vander."

"Aye, Sir," came the instant response.

"It appears the wind is rising outside ... engage the shuttle's hurricane magnets."

"Copy that, Captain."

Jax's frown slid into a scowl as he cut the call. Now that he was alone, with only a droid for company, he could let his mask slip. The High Priestess hadn't mentioned the high winds and storms. She probably hoped a twister would cut its way across the landing platform and take his shuttle with it.

The damned woman was going to obstruct him at every turn.

"Your drink, Captain."

Jax took the tumbler from the droid, favoring it with a curt nod. Lights blinking, it turned and rolled back to its charging station on the wall. "I'm here if you require anything else," it chirped.

Lifting the glass to his lips, Jax took a measured sip. Liquid fire burned across his tongue and down his throat.

He welcomed it, turning back to the view once more.

The light here was eerie. He'd known that the Temple of the Gods sat in perpetual dusk, and had been ready for it, but now that he was here, he wondered how those who lived on this planet for years put up with the murk.

When the call had gone up throughout the sector for applicants for the Guardians of the Flame, he'd put his name forward without hesitation. He'd reached the apex of his career, but it wasn't enough.

He wanted a challenge, and he'd found it.

Jax had always been ambitious. Leading the Mir-Lelith special forces had been an honor, but he wanted to be remembered for something. He wanted to leave his mark. All his life, he'd worked hard, but felt he'd never gotten the credit he was owed.

This mission would change that.

Taking another sip of whisky, his jaw tightened. The High Priestess was being deliberately obtuse. Even living on this isolated rock, she'd know *The Creed of Truth* was a real danger to the sector these days. Just six months earlier, they'd made an attempt on the Mir-Ferrin clan-lord's life.

Frustration boiled up within Jax then. *The Creed* had to be stopped before they destroyed the fragile balance of power within the sector, leaving a vacuum they'd be only too happy to fill.

A chiming sound resonated through the temple then, rising above the howl of the wind.

Jax turned toward the sound. "What's that?" he asked his droid.

"The tolling happens regularly, Sir," it replied, lights fluttering to life on its domed head. "It creates a routine for those who live inside the temple. That one was the Eighteenth Chime, which means it is time for supper."

Nodding, Jax raised the tumbler to his lips and drained the last of his whisky. That made sense. Surrounded by perpetual dusk, time seemed to stand still on this planet. The bells would provide a semblance of structure, a day of sorts, for those who lived here.

"Right," he said, placing his glass on the window ledge. "I'd better go downstairs."

4. AN OPPRESSIVE PRESENCE

"ALLOWING THEM HERE was a big mistake," Ava muttered.

Walking next to her, as they made their way down a wide corridor toward the dining hall, Sister Skylar's usually serene expression tightened. "Really?"

"Yes, I can feel it in my gut." Ava sought to soften her tone then. Raging inwardly was one thing—although she needed to rid herself of the outrage that now bubbled inside her—yet showing anger was another matter.

It was not their way.

"So that threat isn't real?"

"No … it's real," Ava admitted, her pulse quickening. "Although the Guardians of the Flame could bring about our downfall before *The Creed* ever reaches us."

Skylar's dark eyes widened. "Will you go before the Wise Ones and complain?"

"I just might."

Skylar's throat worked, as she tried to maintain her own outward façade of calm. Ava and Skylar had arrived on Pillarus One, just a week apart, years earlier, and had been close friends ever since. Skylar was one of the most senior priestesses and Ava's Second. And should anything happen to the High Priestess, she would likely step into the role.

"I haven't seen any of the warriors yet," Skylar admitted after a lengthy pause. "I've spent most of the day meditating."

"Well, brace yourself. It's a shock."

"Why?"

Ava pulled a face. "You'll see what I mean soon enough," she replied ominously.

Her friend's gaze held hers. "Did their captain offend you?"

Ava's jaw clenched, and she managed a jerky nod. "He marched straight in here and started telling me about all the changes he's going to make." She paused then, her anger spiking once more. Choking it down, she continued, "He carried weapons before the altar … before telling me that those on the Watch must be armed in the future."

Skylar's face went rigid. And despite that her coppery skin hid her emotions more than Ava's pale complexion did, Ava could have sworn she paled. "Didn't he know that weapons are forbidden inside the chapel?"

"Probably. Don't worry, I reminded him … but he didn't care. He told me things will have to change."

Skylar blinked as if she wasn't sure she'd heard correctly. "How dare he?"

"I told you," Ava replied with a shake of her head. "The man is trouble."

Letting these words lie, she strode toward the archway leading into the dining hall.

The Eighteenth Chime had sung around ten minutes earlier, and the High Priestess and her Second were the last to arrive. Ava had been too busy pacing around her chamber, ranting to Dee Dee, to heed the tolling of the supper bell. It was only when Skylar knocked on her door that she realized she was late.

And dammit, not only were all her sisters already seated, their backs ramrod straight, their expressions startled, but they were staring with fascination at Captain Jax's team.

Extra tables had been brought in to accommodate the twenty marines. To her surprise, there were a couple of female warriors among them—tall, broad-shouldered human women who held themselves with supreme self-confidence. And both the male and female Guardians of the Flame observed the staring priestesses with predatory intensity.

Despite that they were all seated for supper, Captain Jax's team appeared alert, ready to jump into action in an instant if required.

Ava's heart started pounding. Both sides were showing far too much interest in each other.

This was what I was afraid of.

The Sisters of Awe lived in austerity, in seclusion, for a reason. She'd feared the arrival of these warriors would be a distraction from their focus on keeping the communication between mortals and the Gods strong and unsullied—and she was right.

She noted then that Captain Jax wasn't seated with his warriors. Instead, he stood upon the dais above the hall, next to the table where Ava took her meals.

He was waiting for her.

Skylar murmured a soft prayer under her breath, her step slowing.

It was a bitter irony that the greatest distraction so far was not to her sisters, but herself.

"I told you," Ava muttered. "He thinks he's in charge here."

At the sight of the two women's entrance, the priestesses and the warriors stopped eyeballing each other; instead, all gazes snapped to Ava and Skylar.

There was an air of nervous excitement in the hall this evening. Their peaceful, carefully controlled existence had been shattered. It would take days for the priestesses to settle.

Trying to ignore the fact she was sweating, Ava drew her shoulders back and swept by the long tables, past the warriors seated there. Meanwhile, Skylar silently made her way over to her place at one of the tables on the main floor.

Ava stepped up onto the dais and favored Captain Jax with a stiff nod. "Captain," she greeted him, her tone clipped. "There's no need to stand on ceremony. You can sit down with your warriors now."

"I won't be dining with them, My Lady," he replied, his voice low and smooth. "At mealtimes, I will be seated with you." Ava's gaze snapped wide at this announcement, yet he continued. "Good communication between the two of us is important ... and mealtimes will allow me to learn more about how this order is run."

Ava's pulse started to race at this declaration, it was only with iron will that she prevented her reaction from showing on her face. Once again, the captain's high-handed manner made her blood pressure rise.

How dare he stride in here and tell her where he would sit at mealtimes? He had no right, at all.

But the eyes of the whole dining hall were on her now, and she could not bring shame upon them or herself by losing her temper.

Center yourself. Breathe.

So, as much as she wanted to step forward, get in the captain's face, and stab her finger into his chest while telling him he wasn't welcome at her table, she refrained.

Slowly counting to ten, she moved to her seat and lowered herself down onto it. Wordlessly, Captain Jax sat down next to her. Their seats had been placed close, close enough that their elbows could brush accidentally.

Heat washed over Ava. Had he moved their seats together? It was as if he was trying to deliberately provoke her at every turn, and she was sick of it. Once supper was over, she was going to have to see about curtailing his authoritarian behavior.

The squeak of rubber wheels on polished stone drew Ava's attention then, and she looked up to see a small army of utility-droids trundling into the hall. Each of them carried a platter with bowls of vegetable stew and piles of flat-bread.

The sulfurous smell of the stew drifted across the hall. Droids prepared all the meals here. The dishes were always simple and largely plant-based. Supplies were brought in from the nearest habitable system, and they used Mir-Brennan food replicators for the shortfall. However, fresh food was always preferable.

The droids delivered Ava and the captain's meals to their table, and then the pair silently began to eat.

And as soon as the high priestess and her companion started their meal, the priestesses and the warriors seated below the dais followed suit.

Ava ate slowly, deliberately. Her stomach had closed, and she felt a little nauseated. Food was the last thing she wanted right now, but under the watchful eye of all, she needed to keep her composure.

And all the while, she was acutely aware of Captain Jax's oppressive presence at her side. She expected him to break the brittle silence between them, to start questioning her about the running of this temple. But he didn't.

After a while, she found herself stealing glances his way. The captain had removed his heavy plate armor, although he was no less formidable and intimidating wearing the close-fitting black body suit underneath. She'd expected him to look somewhat diminished without that bulky armor, yet thick muscle packed his body. Upon his chest, he wore a badge: a golden flame with eight stars ringed above it—symbolizing the sacred flame and the eight High Gods.

Ava's pulse quickened. It was the same one that she wore over her heart.

Heat flushed over her once more. *He sits at my table and wears the sacred seal,* she thought incredulously. *He thinks we're equals.*

Her gaze shifted then, traveling down to where his hand reached for more bread.

Earlier, Captain Jax had been wearing gloves, but now he'd removed them, revealing large yet well-sculpted hands. However, when she saw the curved black fingernails that tipped his blunt fingers, Ava stilled. They were short and well-kept, yet they weren't human.

"So, you've noticed I'm half Vulkar, have you?"

Ava's gaze snapped up, her cheeks burning. Shit. He'd caught her staring. Swallowing, she brazened the moment out. "Yes." She looked up into his face, and this time the obsidian depths of his eyes, so black she couldn't separate the pupils from the irises, and his heavy brow, made sense. He'd favored the human side a little more than the Vulkar one, although now that she viewed him closely, she was surprised she hadn't noticed earlier.

Ava's attention shifted then to the two tables where the captain's team sat. One of them was a full-blooded Vulkar—a huge bald male with sallow skin, a prominent brow-ridge, and glittering eyes the color of a space field. Inky talons tipped thick fingers. The warrior wasn't the only non-human among the group. A green-skinned, gilled Daksari and a lizard-faced Rendak sat amongst them.

She'd had little to do with Vulkar over the years. However, their aggression and volcanic tempers were well-known. No wonder Captain Jax had stridden in here like he owned the place. Vulkar were dominant, especially with females.

Jaw clenched, she shifted her gaze away from the Guardians of the Flame and focused on her meal once more. Nonetheless, she felt the captain's gaze upon her. He expected her to say something, and she was going to have to humor him.

Maybe if they conversed, the rage that was burning a hole in her stomach would settle. Straight after supper, she'd go up to her solar and meditate. She wanted her peace back.

"Where are you from, Captain?" she asked after a heavy pause.

"Morvin."

Her brow furrowed. "In the Yariz System?"

"Yes."

It was the nearest habitable system to this one.

She glanced his way once more to find him watching her under hooded lids. "You will have noticed the temple is paved in Morvinian marble."

"I did … there's no mistaking the stone," he answered. "And the statues of the Eight are sculpted from it too."

"They are." Another awkward silence fell between them.

"And where do you hail from, My Lady?" he asked eventually.

Gods, this conversation was awkward.

"I grew up on a mining moon … Morith."

"Where the best whisky in the sector comes from."

She cut him a sidelong look. "That's right. I was a governor's daughter."

He raised a heavy eyebrow. "Was? Are your family dead then?"

"I wouldn't know." She looked away as an old ache rose under her breastbone—a reminder of all she'd given up for this order. "I haven't had any contact with them in years. Once you join the Sisters of Awe, you sever all ties with your old life."

"How long have you lived here?"

Ava tensed. She didn't mind answering one or two questions, but this was starting to feel like an interrogation. "Fifteen years."

"And I hear you are the youngest High Priestess in nearly two centuries?"

She nodded.

The captain picked up a cup of water and took a sip. "Your accession was abrupt."

"It was." Ava knew where this conversation was heading, but she couldn't stop it. The subject was bound to come up sooner or later.

"I read the official report on Lady Keisha's death … but found it vague," he continued, confirming her suspicions. "It said she passed away 'suddenly'?"

"She did."

Ava took another mouthful of stew and forced herself to swallow it. And all the while, he watched her. Vulkar were known for their penetrating stares too—something that worked in their favor during negotiations. "What happened to her?"

Huffing a sigh, Ava sat back in her chair and cut him an irritated glance. "Lady Keisha had been unwell for a while before her death ... her mental health had declined. The medic-droid was treating her for depression and anxiety, but it was worse than we realized. One day, while the rest of us were sleeping, she left the temple unescorted and traveled on foot to the dark side of the planet." Ava paused there, remembering that awful day. She hated to recall what had happened to Keisha. "Ice-crawlers got her before she'd walked two klicks in ... although the lack of oxygen and the cold would have killed her if they hadn't."

Captain Jax's expression grew grave. "You'd better tell me about these 'ice-crawlers'," he said, his black eyes narrowing.

Ava picked up her cup, cradling it with both hands. "There isn't much to say," she replied. "They're large arachnids that live on the dark side and rarely stray beyond it." She shuddered, recalling seeing the glistening white insects crouching over Keisha's crumpled body, feeding off her. Ava had been inside the bubble cockpit of an all-terrain hopper, speeding toward them.

Spying her approach, the ice-crawlers had given outraged squeals and scuttled off, long limbs flailing.

Oxygen mask in place, and clumsily gripping a stun-wand, she'd drawn up the hopper and leaped out, Skylar at her side. But it had been too late for Keisha.

"So, they aren't usually a problem?"

Ava shook her head. "The terminator has narrowed over the centuries ... and the temperature in this zone has dropped. Occasionally ice-crawlers venture into the twilight, although it's rare."

The captain took this in, his expression inscrutable. "Even so, I will have my team carry out regular patrols on the dark edge of this zone," he replied. "Anything else I should be aware of? Severe storms, for example?"

Ava tensed, catching the edge in his voice. So, someone had told him about the regular hurricanes that swept across this planet, had they?

She chose to ignore the jibe. Once again, his authoritarian tone made her hackles rise. "A few rodents and insects live here, but most of them are harmless," she replied shifting her attention to her supper once more.

Having this man at her side at mealtimes was going to wreak havoc with her digestion.

A loud 'boom' rang across the dining hall then, followed by the grinding sound of metal.

Her dining companion jolted in his seat, while at the tables below, his warriors jerked upright, their gazes snapping toward the sound.

However, the priestesses kept eating, as did Ava.

"What is that?" Captain Jax growled as the sound continued.

"The hurricane shutters are closing," Ava replied calmly, although not without a little satisfaction. She'd enjoyed seeing these intruders startled by something she and her sisters were used to by now. The arrival of the Guardians might have unsettled them, yet the frequent hurricanes that plagued this planet didn't. "When the wind rises above thirty-five knots, the shutters automatically seal." She glanced his way then. "We'll be in for a rough night."

5. SHATTERING THE SILENCE

AND IT *WAS* a rough night—for Ava, at least.

It wasn't the hurricane that bothered her. In the years she'd lived here, there had been many. The order had established weather stations throughout the twilight zone and usually had warning. As such, she'd known hours ago that a strong one was coming, but she hadn't bothered to tell Captain Jax.

Ava wasn't going to volunteer information. She didn't want him here and wasn't going to make things easy for him or his team. She didn't want to anger the Wise Ones. However, she just wasn't going to smooth his path and prostrate herself so he could wipe his heavy boots on her.

Captain Jax had looked disgruntled earlier, as the booming and clanging of the Lazda Steel shutters closing over the exterior of the temple and the towers that ringed it echoed through the hall. He liked to be in control, that much was clear, and didn't appreciate her keeping things back from him.

"Get used to it, asshole," Ava snarled as she paced around her bedchamber, her bare feet whispering on polished stone. Her meditation session after supper had calmed her—but the second she was alone in her bedchamber, anger resurfaced.

She shouldn't be cursing like this. It wasn't seemly at all, yet it gave her a small measure of freedom in a life that sometimes felt as if it was suffocating her.

From the moment she rose, just before the Sixth Chime, to when she finally retired after an evening meditation session in her solar, Ava's days were tightly structured. Before breakfast, she led a morning service. Then, once they'd eaten, she took the novices through their daily scripture and history lessons. The High

Priestess was also expected to visit the chapel every three chimes, to offer prayers and check that the those guarding the flame weren't shirking their duties. And on top of all that, she had to spend hours studying the history of their order, researching ways to better serve the Galactic Gods.

The tolling of the bell ruled Ava's life, and sometimes, when she lay awake while the rest of the temple slept, she wondered if she'd made the right choice all those years ago.

In truth, the arrival of the Guardians of the Flame unsettled her on many levels. In just one day, they'd shattered the silence, the delicate equilibrium of her existence.

Her exchange with Captain Jax at supper, and talking about her past, had reminded her of the wide-eyed postulant she'd once been. Although she hadn't admitted such to him, moving here hadn't been easy.

In the beginning, she'd missed her family—even her aloof father. Although it was a privilege to be accepted into the Sisters of Awe, Ava's elder sisters had been bemused by her decision. A life of seclusion wasn't for everyone.

And indeed, in her first weeks here, Ava was sure she'd made a terrible mistake. She'd always been devout, taking her mother's lead, and had been excited to become a sister—but the silence, the isolation, the relentless wind, and low-light levels, had all gotten to her initially, as had the rigid daily routine they all had to adhere to.

She'd cried silently on her bunk in the darkness while her sisters slept around her, yet said nothing. And slowly, as the weeks slid into months, the despair that sat like an asteroid in her belly lightened. Slowly, she came to accept that this was her life.

This was what she'd wanted, what she'd asked for. It was too late to have regrets now—and ungrateful too, for what greater honor was there than to serve the gods?

No, it hadn't been easy, and in many ways, it still wasn't.

Her thoughts drifted back from the past then, returning to the overbearing individual who had just torn a hole in her orderly world.

Already, she'd spent far too much time with Captain Jax; it had taken her from her duties and made her lose focus. But her stomach twisted when she realized this was just the beginning.

It was Day One, and she wanted him gone.

"It is late, Mistress," Dee Dee's metallic voice intruded then. "Do you want me to run you a bath before bed?"

Ava ceased her pacing and turned to her droid. Dee Dee observed her from its docking station on the wall. She'd thought the utility-droid had shut down for the 'night', but it seemed her constant circling and muttering had woken it up.

"Yes, thank you, Dee Dee," she sighed. She loved her baths—and needed to relax.

Light blinking, DD-J3 rolled away into the adjoining bathroom. Moments later, the soothing sound of rushing water reached her.

Ava started to disrobe. And as she did so, she caught sight of herself in the full-length mirror on the wall.

Her reflection made her still for a moment. Gods, she looked strained.

She was only thirty-three, yet tonight, she seemed older. The furrowed brow and mouth turned down in disapproval didn't help things. Scrubbing her hands through her short white-blonde hair, she winced.

Keisha had aged faster than she should have in this role—maybe Ava would too.

Maybe you'll lose your mind like she did.

Queasiness rolled over her then. She didn't want to think about that. Yet sometimes the worry would pop up unbidden, causing dread to curl in the pit of her belly. Stepping into the role of High Priestess was an honor indeed. Nonetheless, it came at a cost for each woman who wore the mantle; Ava wondered what price she'd have to pay.

Trying to ignore the worry that tugged at her, Ava shrugged out of her robes. The paleness of her naked skin was almost blinding in the mirror. Her gaze narrowed then as she ran a critical eye over her body.

Whether or not she was physically attractive didn't matter.

She'd dedicated her life to the Gods, and they didn't care what she looked like.

Even so, there was a traitorous part of her that wished she was beautiful—like her two elder blood-sisters were. Unlike Helia and Yarla, who were slender and small, their younger sister was sturdily built and towered over most men. And unlike them, she had an unfashionably large bust—which the flowing robes she wore emphasized rather than hid—making it look like the prow of a ship.

Ironically, standing next to Captain Jax today was the first time she'd *ever* felt small and feminine. He stood head and shoulders over her.

Swearing under her breath, for the last thing she needed was to keep thinking about the aggravating individual, Ava turned away from the mirror and her reflection and walked naked through to the bathroom. The bath was nearly ready, and Dee Dee was pouring some scented oil into it.

"It's ready, mistress," the droid chirped, rolling past, and making for the door.

Gingerly stepping into the steaming water, Ava lowered herself into the tub. The utility-droid knew exactly how she liked her bath.

With another, deep, sigh, she leaned back, resting her head on the ledge behind her and letting the hot water soak into her limbs.

That's better.

Her gaze went to the window. Of course, the Lazda hurricane shutters obscured the view, which was a shame, for she enjoyed looking out across the craggy landscape to where one of the planet's three moons hung low in the sky. Nonetheless, she could hear the wind clawing at the metal, shrieking around the eaves.

In her first days here, the storms *had* unsettled her, had stretched her nerves tight. Sometimes they would go on for days, and the whine of the wind would affect them all, causing tempers to fray and arguments among the sisters—something that was usually rare.

Inhaling the floral scent that drifted up from the water, Ava closed her eyes.

And as the seconds slid by, her anger and tension started to dissolve.

Enough ruminating about the arrival of the Guardians of Flame or worrying about the disruptions they'd cause in the temple.

Right now, she was going to focus on enjoying her bath.

"Are the proximity beacons all in place?"

"Yes, Captain … if there are any intruders, they'll let us know."

Jax's mouth thinned. The beacons all contained the latest tech, but that didn't mean they were infallible. "Have you scouted the entire terminator yet?"

First Officer Vander Mir-Riorde nodded his head, his sharp dark-blue gaze meeting Jax's. "Everything checks out, Sir."

"No ice-crawlers?" Even the name of those arachnids that lived on the dark side of the planet caused Jax's skin to prickle.

"Not one."

The two men had met outside the entrance to the temple. The hurricane had passed, leaving a breathless calm in its wake. The air, as usual, was cool, although the lack of life surrounding them put Jax on edge. He'd grown up on a planet where you could hear the chatter of birds and the rustling of leaves whenever you stepped outside.

"This planet really is dying," he muttered, voicing his thoughts aloud.

Vander's brow furrowed. "Yeah … it's an eerie place." He halted then, his gaze sweeping the rocky valley below the temple. "I was reading up about Pillarus One last night … can you believe that eons ago, thick forests covered this world?"

Jax shook his head. No, he couldn't—although, he knew what the passing of ages did to planets. It was a stark reminder that death came to them all, even planets and stars. Nothing in the universe lived forever, not even the cosmos itself.

The realization made his gut tense. He didn't like being faced with his insignificance in the scheme of things. It was unnerving.

The two men began walking then, making their way along the thin path that snaked around the base of the temple.

"Have you spoken to the High Priestess again?" Vander asked after a minute or two, breaking the silence between them.

Jax shook his head. After yesterday's 'discussions,' he wanted to give the woman time to cool down, to get used to the new status quo.

"She's going to fight you, isn't she?"

Jax cast his first officer a sidelong glance. "She can try, but the clan leaders have given us permission to do what's necessary to protect this order … as have the Wise Ones." His gaze lifted then to where the Tower of Flame rose above the temple's domed roof. "If they have spoken, the High Priestess has to obey."

"I saw the way she was glaring at you during supper, Sir." Vander's voice held a slightly amused edge now. "You'd better keep any sharp objects away from Lady Ava when you hit her with the rest of your news."

Jax snorted. He wasn't afraid of one self-important woman. Even a High Priestess wasn't beyond reproach. Ava Mir-Brennan would do as she was told.

They continued walking, falling into silence once more. After hours of screaming wind, the stillness seemed unnatural. In the distance, Jax caught sight of one of their silver hoppers streaking through a deep valley on its way north. There was a place of pilgrimage—a towering mountain top where the Sky Altar sat, around a day's journey from here—where the priestesses visited for the yearly Blood Rite. The ceremony was still over two months away, but all the same, he'd sent some of his men up to ensure the site was secure.

In the meantime, *The Star-Hawk* continued to orbit the planet, and Commander Asher had set up a security net. They'd know if anyone approached Pillarus One or attempted to land on the planet without permission.

Jax's wrist-comm buzzed then, and he glanced down to see that Commander Asher onboard the light cruiser was hailing him.

"Commander," he greeted him curtly.

"Captain. We've just had word that there's been an attack on Morvin. Key government buildings have been destroyed, as have temples to Jidea and Syr. There's been considerable loss of life ... and *The Creed* has claimed responsibility for it."

Vander breathed a curse. Meanwhile, Jax went still. A moment later, his pulse started thudding in his ears. Morvin. His home. It was a peaceful planet, with little to draw the notice of the rest of the sector except for the marble mined there. It was an easy target.

"How?" he growled.

"They placed pyro-detonators in the capital, Sir ... and set them off remotely. No one's been arrested, and there have been no leads."

"Fuck."

Jax wasn't worried about his family. His father no longer lived on Morvin, and his mother didn't reside in the capital. However, Yariz was the closest habitable system to Pillarus One.

The threat was drawing uncomfortably close.

"They're growing in strength," Vander said quietly, casting a glance around them as if he expected missiles to rain down from the sky.

Jax huffed out an angry breath. "We need reinforcements," he admitted after a lengthy pause. It was true. The clan leaders had given him a team of seventy warriors, twenty of whom were on-planet while the rest waited aboard *The Star-Hawk*. He had enough to keep watch on the temple, yet he wanted the security to be watertight—especially with *The Creed* this close. "I shall put in a request for another cruiser, more weapons … and more warriors."

"Good idea, Sir," Asher replied. "But, in the meantime, this planet is secure."

"Yeah," Jax muttered. "For the moment."

6. TRAINING BEGINS

AVA WALKED ACROSS the temple floor, her gaze sweeping over the wide space to where two of her sisters stood rigidly to attention before the sacred flame.

Their faces were taut, their gazes narrowed as they stared ahead.

Slowing her step, Ava's attention rested on the laser-pistols both priestesses now carried strapped to their hips.

Her mouth thinned, her stomach twisting. Why were her sisters already carrying weapons? They didn't even know how to use them.

It was an abomination, one which risked incurring the wrath of the Gods.

But Captain Jax didn't seem to care. It infuriated her that she didn't have the authority to prevent the Guardians of the Flame from arming the Watch. She'd even sent the Wise Ones a message the night before, warning them of the captain's sacrilegious behavior—but they hadn't yet replied.

Halting before the altar, Ava lowered herself onto one knee and genuflected before placing both palms flat on the cool pavers in a position of prayer. It was early evening, and supper was approaching. Eyes closed, she whispered to each of the Eight in turn, honoring them as she did many times a day. Meanwhile, the two priestesses on the Watch, one of which was Skylar, remained standing, impassive, and as still as the statues that lined this space.

However, it was difficult for Ava to keep focused.

Of course, all her sisters were on edge right now. Captain Jax had informed everyone about the attack on Morvin when they'd sat down to lunch in the dining hall. The news had sent a ripple of alarm through the rows of priestesses seated below the dais. It was a bold strike on a peaceful world.

Ava was annoyed that he'd stood up and made such an announcement, without speaking to her privately first. The priestesses couldn't fulfill their duties—guarding the sacred flame, cleaning the chapel, prayer, study, and meditation—if they were distracted.

But beneath her anger, fear had risen at learning about what *The Creed* had done on Morvin. The extremist group was growing stronger, bolder. Ava's spine prickled as she tried to concentrate on her prayers. Would they really come for her? Captain Jax insisted that, as the mortal conduit to the Gods, she was a target.

And what better way to weaken the power of the Eight than to strike here, in a place where all the Galactic Gods were revered equally?

Ava inhaled deeply. Enough. She was letting emotion swamp her these days, and it was beginning to compromise her. Anger and fear couldn't dominate a High Priestess's mind, for she couldn't communicate with the Gods with such emotions boiling within her.

She had to regain her equilibrium.

Pushing her worries aside, Ava doggedly continued her prayers. Eventually, a little of the tension in her belly eased. Prayer never failed to calm her. This practice was a reminder that there were some things *The Creed of Truth* could never change. There wasn't just one God, but many.

The Creed could lay waste to this sector and burn every temple and shrine to the ground, but they'd never succeed in making Wis the only deity. The citizens of the Rith Sector would just conduct their worship in secret.

Ava's breathing grew shallow as she rose to her feet and genuflected once more. All the same, if *The Creed* achieved its goal, the resulting chaos would be terrible.

Leaving the chapel, she made her way through a network of stark corridors. The Eighteenth Chime had just echoed through the temple, which meant it was time for supper. Ava walked briskly to the dining hall. She wanted to get there before Captain Jax did, to prepare herself for his unsettling and aggravating company.

A scattering of priestesses was there already, seated at the long tables, their gazes on the doorway. Some of them blushed and averted their gazes when Ava strode in, as if she had caught them out.

She had.

They were watching for the Guardians.

Ava made her way across to them.

"Good evening, Lady Ava," the priestesses chorused, rising from their seats, and bowing their heads respectfully.

Ava gestured for them to sit. "Remember what I warned you about before the Guardians of the Flame arrived," she greeted them without preamble. "Your purpose here is to honor the Gods. If you find yourself distracted, you must confine yourself to your quarters and meditate until you find your focus again ... is that clear?"

The sisters all nodded, even as their blushes deepened.

"You must treat the newcomers like shadows. You are not to interact with them" —she shot Yinna, the youngest and most guilty-looking of the group a censorious look— "or encourage them to interact with you." Ava paused then, letting her words sink in, before adding. "Any of you who disregard this will be sent to the crypt for solitary contemplation."

Their faces stiffened, eyes widening. It was a harsh punishment. The crypt under the temple was a dark, gloomy place. In the past, it had been used to confine misbehaving priestesses, but neither Ava nor her predecessor had ever sent anyone there. She didn't add that she, or any of her priestesses, would be expulsed from the order if she broke the oath of chastity she'd sworn before the Gods. Some things were clear.

A heavy silence fell before Yinna's girlish voice echoed across the hall. "But you talk to their captain, My Lady. Why must we avoid them while you don't?"

The other priestesses shot their companion a horrified look, yet Yinna ignored them. Small and fragile-looking, with doe-like eyes and flyaway white-blonde hair the same color as Ava's, she held the High Priestess's eye boldly.

Ava stilled, taking care to keep her expression carefully veiled. Yinna had arrived as a postulant six months earlier and had just taken her vows. Nonetheless, she questioned everything about life here, much as Ava herself once had. "I speak to him out of necessity, Sister Yinna, and for no other reason," she replied sternly.

Disappointment shadowed Yinna's brown eyes, yet she bowed her head in submission.

Ava frowned. She wasn't yet done making her point, yet crimson-robed figures were now filtering into the hall. She'd have to call Yinna to her solar and speak to her privately later. It was clear the novice was struggling with the rules.

Nodding curtly to the priestesses she'd just reprimanded, Ava turned and walked down the length of the long hall. Pink light filtered in from the high windows, illuminating the dust motes that floated above. The dining hall was one of her favorite places within the temple, although if she was honest, she'd preferred it when she'd been able to sit amongst her sisters.

She'd always glanced up at the dais, at where Keisha ate alone, and thought she cut a lonely figure.

Maybe it was loneliness that pushed her over the edge.

Pushing aside the unsettling sensation that always accompanied thoughts of Keisha, Ava stepped up onto the dais and moved over to where two places had been set at the table. With a quick look at the doors, she deftly moved Captain Jax's cutlery and chair a few inches farther from her.

As much as she longed for company while she ate her meals, *he* wasn't her choice. Instead, she wished Skylar would join her. Ever since she'd stepped into Keisha's role—selected by the Wise Ones themselves— the two friends had spent increasingly less time together.

Ava settled herself down at the table and tried to ignore the heaviness that now pressed upon her breastbone.

She *was* lonely—there was no denying it. These days, her longest conversations were with Dee Dee, her droid.

And Captain Jax.

The doors to the hall slid open then, drawing her eye.

Tall, broad-shouldered figures swaggered in. Like the day before, the Guardians had removed their plate armor before entering the dining hall. But they were all imposing, nonetheless. And as Ava had expected, their attention swept the hall to where Yinna and her friends sat.

Ava's gaze bored into the sisters, daring any of them to meet the marines' stares.

They didn't.

The captain himself strode in at the heels of his warriors. His expression was austere—his heavy brow furrowed, his jaw set—as he strode down the aisle between the tables and headed for the dais.

And although Ava had told the priestesses not to watch the guardians, she found herself tracking his approach.

The day before, she'd found his stance predatory as he'd stepped out of his shuttle—and today, she marked his stalking gait, the way the heavy muscles under the close-fitting body suit rippled and bunched as he walked.

Her pulse fluttered, her palms growing damp.

A sickly sensation swiftly followed. Was she *attracted* to him?

The Gods forgive her, she'd been so busy clashing with Captain Jax that she hadn't realized she was also keenly aware of him.

Ava's heart started to pound. She'd just lectured her sisters on keeping their distance from the Guardians, and here she was, reacting physically to their leader—a man she couldn't stand.

She was a hypocrite.

"My Lady," Captain Jax greeted her, sliding into his chair.

"Captain."

Meanwhile, the hall was filling up as the rest of the priestesses arrived from different corners of the temple. Only the two on the Watch would remain at their posts, along with the warriors on patrol at the doors—and they would all eat later.

The rise and fall of voices, male and female, drifted through the dining hall.

"You will have noticed I have armed the Watch," the captain said without preamble.

Ava clenched her jaw. "I did," she bit out. "Isn't it dangerous to give weapons to those who don't know how to use them?"

"It is," he replied, those unsettling obsidian eyes spearing her. "And that's why we'll be teaching your priestesses how to defend themselves, with weapons and with their fists." His mouth, usually a hard slash, softened then, into what might have been a smile. "Training starts tomorrow."

A cool, dusty wind whistled across the terrace, stirring the robes of the priestesses lined up there.

Standing back from them, arms folded across her chest, Ava bristled in mutinous silence.

This was yet another offense to the Gods. Their order was peaceful. They didn't need to learn how to hurt and kill others.

And from the looks on many of her sisters' faces, they agreed. Many of them were frowning, and they kept glancing the High Priestess's way as if she could save them.

She couldn't, it seemed.

They were all dressed in their long, sleeveless red tunics this morning, belted at the waist, and had shed their cloaks. Their gazes warily followed the captain as he strode up and down the terrace, eying them.

He was dressed in full armor and wearing his visored helmet. Red and black shone, even in the dull light, and his crimson cloak fluttered in the breeze.

Three of his team stood behind him, also armored and visored.

They were a threatening sight, and Ava couldn't help but think it was deliberate. They didn't mean to put the sisters at ease.

"You're dealing with terrorists," the captain told them, his low baritone rolling across the terrace like thunder. "They have this temple in their sights and will be planning how to destroy it, even as we speak."

Ava's skin prickled. Damn him, did he need to be so blunt?

One or two of the priestesses had started to sweat; Ava could see the gleam on their brows.

"You need to learn how to defend yourselves," Captain Jax continued. "We're going to start with hand-to-hand combat this morning ... but within the next few days, we'll progress to using a laser-pistol and blade. Your training will be rigorous. Usually, these skills take months to learn." He paused, his visored gaze sweeping the line of red-clad women. "We don't have months."

He whirled, his red cloak billowing in the wind. "Right ... you need to get into a fighting stance. Think of your feet as the roots that keep your body in place. You need to be grounded, or you'll be easy to knock over. Now, extend your non-dominant foot toward me and move your other foot behind you, about a shoulder-width back." He paused, watching as the priestesses all shuffled into position. "When you move, do so on the balls of your feet ... you'll be faster."

Ava remained on the edge of the terrace, looking on while the captain instructed them how to hold their torso, head, and arms. She'd never realized that self-defense used the whole body. Granted, all the priestesses appeared a bit ungainly as they self-consciously moved into the right position. However, that would soon change.

Despite herself, Ava was riveted. Her world was so narrow here, it felt odd to widen her perspective. And despite that she didn't want her sisters to learn to fight or handle weapons, there was a small, traitorous part of her that was envious they were being trained, and not her. Over the past couple of days, she'd found herself stealing glances at the female warriors in Captain Jax's team—and wondering what it would feel like to be that strong, that confident.

Once the captain was satisfied with the preliminaries, he called in his lieutenant, a tall, lean human male called Vander. The man was covered, head-to-toe, in armor this morning, but the day before, Ava had noted that he had a handsome, if sharp-featured, face and a shock of auburn hair, which he wore tied back at the nape of his neck. There, the two of them demonstrated the first techniques of self-defense while the priestesses looked on.

"If you're being attacked, don't just stand there with your fists up," Captain Jax explained. Despite his heavy armor and well-muscled physique, he shifted lightly from side to side on the balls of his feet while Vander struck at him with gloved fists. "It's much harder to hit a moving target. Keep your back straight, your stomach muscles engaged, and maintain eye contact with your opponent."

He showed them how to defend themselves from punches then, before teaching them how to land strikes of their own without breaking fingers or shattering their wrists.

Then he split the priestesses up into pairs and left Vander to take over while he stepped back, viewing the sparring for a few moments.

His visored gaze swept right, to where Ava still stood, watching the practice.

She tensed, her brow furrowing as he strode around the edge of the platform toward her. And as he approached, Ava started to sweat.

The Gods give her strength. She needed to stop reacting like this every time the captain walked her way.

Raising her chin and keeping her arms folded to create a barrier between them, she eyed him. The captain stopped in front of her, and then to her consternation, flipped up his visor. "My Lady," he greeted her.

"Captain." She cleared her throat then. "So, will my sisters make good fighters?"

"That remains to be seen," he replied, his black gaze settling upon her. "They take instruction well … so that's a start." He paused then, his head inclining. "But they're not the only ones who need to learn to fight." Ava's pulse kicked into hyperdrive as he continued. "Come with me, My Lady … your training begins now too."

7. THWARTED

STAGGERING BACK, AVA brought up an arm to deflect Captain Jax's heavy blow. His naked fist slammed against her forearm.

"Raise your arms higher and cup your hands at eye level," he instructed. "You're not protecting your face … and twist like I showed you."

His heavy fist came at her again, and this time Ava swiveled, letting his knuckles graze along the underside of her upper arm.

"That's better," he grunted.

The captain withdrew then, his dark brows drawing together as he observed her.

Breathing hard, Ava watched him. This would teach her to secretly envy her sisters their training. She didn't any longer.

They stood in the conservatory, the only place with enough space to practice where they wouldn't be interrupted or observed. The High Priestess had a certain standing within the temple—it would go against protocol for her to train out in the open where anyone might see her.

Located halfway up the Tower of Flame, with wide circular windows looking out in each direction, the conservatory was a riot of glossy dark-green leaves and ferns. Artificial lights kept the plants alive, as did sprinklers. The air was oxygen-rich and heavy with the smell of foliage and damp earth.

Ava had stripped off her cloak so that, like her sisters, she trained in her long, sleeveless tunic. The attire wasn't ideal, for her skirts kept catching around her legs. The captain had stripped off his plate armor and helmet so that he wore just the black bodysuit underneath.

"I'm going to attack you again," he warned her then. "And this time, I want you to block me with your left arm and strike at my head with your right fist. Make sure your wrist is straight and your thumb is outside your fist, or you'll break it."

Ava snorted. She might not know much about hand-to-hand combat, but even she had heard that. Biting back a sharp retort, she readied herself for his next strike.

He moved toward her, and Ava's heart leaped.

The captain struck at her face, and she blocked him. However, her punch didn't get anywhere near his head.

Frustration boiled up as she danced back on the balls of her feet. The captain was right: it was much easier to move that way.

"There wasn't any power in that punch," he said coolly. "You need to use your whole body when you strike … and follow with your shoulder."

Ava nodded. Curse him. She was wheezing now, yet he didn't even look out of breath.

"All right," she panted. "Let's go again."

And they did. Nonetheless, it took her another four attempts before her knuckles grazed his cheek.

Elation spiked through her as she bounced back, although she was careful to keep her reaction hidden. The asshole might think she was enjoying this—but she wasn't.

Sweat trickled down her back, between her shoulder blades, and the muscles in her upper arms and shoulders were burning.

"Better," Captain Jax said with a nod. However, his expression didn't change. He didn't look impressed by her progress during the session, and she didn't blame him. Most of her sisters whom she'd viewed outside on the terrace had done better.

She really was clumsy, awkward.

Heat prickled her skin as she wondered what was going on behind that inscrutable mask of the man standing in front of her. She hated how he gave nothing away—how, without saying a word, he gave the impression he was the master of this temple and not her.

"Good," she said, her tone clipped. "That's it for now, Captain." Grabbing her cloak from where it hung over the branch of a nearby tree, she headed toward the door. "I have duties awaiting me."

Her dismissal was abrupt, deliberately so. She sensed that their training session was concluded anyway, but she wanted to regain the upper hand; she *needed* to claw back a little dignity and control.

"We'll train daily from now on," he replied. "Meet me here tomorrow morning at the Sixth Chime."

Ava halted abruptly. *Daily?* She then shook her head. "I conduct a service with my sisters at the Sixth Chime … before breakfast."

"Then we shall meet at the Fifth Chime, High Priestess. You must train every morning."

Ava's gaze narrowed. The Fifth Chime was virtually the middle of the night. Gods, she wanted to argue with him. Yet there was a challenge in his voice now, as if he was daring her to do so. The bastard was insinuating she was lazy, but he wouldn't get away with it.

Swallowing her anger, Ava gave a jerky nod, and then, without another word, or a backward glance, she left the conservatory.

Jax watched the High Priestess depart.

And as she did, a rare smile tugged at his lips. He hadn't thought he'd enjoy training Lady Ava, but he had. The woman was a beginner, yet she had grit. He'd found himself wanting to push her harder, just to see how she'd react.

And he would—tomorrow.

The early start didn't bother him. He was used to rising well before any of his warriors did. And Lady Ava would get used to it too.

Moving over to the corner of the conservatory, he picked up his plate armor and fastened it over his bodysuit. It was warm inside this room, uncomfortably so, and he was sweating under the close-fitting material.

This wasn't the ideal place to train, but it was private, which was what the High Priestess demanded.

Carrying his helmet under his arm, Jax left the conservatory and took the narrow winding stairs down to the lower levels of the temple. He could have taken the elevator, as the High Priestess likely had, but he liked to keep his body moving.

He would work out in his room later in the day. Unfortunately, the temple didn't have any recreation facilities. He'd see about changing that. They all needed a place to keep fighting fit.

Below, he passed two of his warriors. They stood ramrod straight at their posts, their visored helmets gleaming in the overhead lights.

"Captain," they both greeted him, slamming their fists over their hearts.

Jax nodded to them, not breaking his stride as he traversed the network of corridors to the chapel. Along the way, he passed a trio of priestesses carrying buckets and mops. They'd obviously just come from cleaning the chapel. Mostly, droids did all the menial duties here, but the chapel was a sacred space—and no droids were permitted entry.

Jax observed the three young priestesses, noting the strain on their faces. The recent changes here were difficult for them to adjust to, and the growing threat presented by *The Creed* had them on edge. The women cast nervous glances at him before hurrying past, gazes downcast.

Entering the quiet chapel beyond, Jax slowed his pace. His gaze swept over the circular space, over the faces of the Eight gathered around the edges, to the two silent figures guarding the sacred flame.

Despite that he saw this temple as his domain now, he never would dare stride through the chapel without pausing and showing some form of reverence. And so, Jax stopped, faced the altar, lowered himself down onto one knee, and bowed his head, whispering a blessing to the Gods.

Upon his world, Syr, the God of Mercy, was the most revered—and as such, he focused on the tall figure of the deity himself, who stood, legs apart, his benevolent face tilted toward the heavens.

Homage paid, Jax then headed across the floor to the network of corridors that led down to the dining hall and kitchens.

During his initial tour, the High Priestess had shown him the kitchens, where a hive of utility-droids worked. She assured him the droids were all serviced regularly, and the food supplies brought in were rigorously checked.

All the same, Jax wasn't convinced. He was looking for weak links, for places where *The Creed* could strike. No food was grown on this planet; everything fresh that the sisters consumed was supplied from off-world. A cargo ship made a drop every thirty days, and the next one was due the following day.

Entering the kitchens, the odor of stewing vegetables hit Jax.

He screwed up his nose. The food here wasn't to his taste. The meals so far consisted of a mushy vegetable stew accompanied by a wedge of cheese and flatbread. If the menu stayed like this, he'd soon start craving a big bloody hunk of steak. Hopefully, the replicator in his chamber could deliver.

Jax's gaze swept the space. Gleaming steel reflected in the overhead lights. No voices filled the kitchen; instead, a symphony of bleeps, beeps, and chirps echoed off the hard surfaces. Droids of varying sizes moved around the kitchen. Some perched at benches, chopping vegetables, knives blurring, while others stirred pots. More droids carted items across the floor.

They seemed to collectively notice Jax.

The flurry of activity halted, as did the cacophony of mechanical noise. The droids swiveled to face him.

Jax stared back a moment before greeting them. "This is a routine inspection." He paused then. "Who's in charge here?"

A tall, thin utility-droid with long, spindly arms started flashing lights upon its cone-shaped head. "I am, Captain," it chirped. "RIC 2S0 at your service."

"Okay, RIC, take me through to the food storage area." Jax wanted to see exactly where and how everything was stored, and if there was anything to be concerned about. *The Creed* would likely target this spot; if he were them, he would.

The droid paused an instant before chirping. "Apologies, Captain, but you have been denied access to the storage area without express permission from the High Priestess."

Jax stiffened. "What?"

"Access is denied," it repeated.

Jax frowned. "To *me* specifically, or everyone?"

More lights flashed on the utility-droid's head. "None of the Guardians of the Flame are permitted." The droid pushed itself away from the bench and strode toward him on spindly metal legs. "I shall escort you out of this restricted area, Captain."

Jax's frown slid into a scowl, "Don't bother," he muttered. "I know the way."

With that, he turned on his heel and strode out of the kitchens.

Lady Ava was deliberately obstructing him. He'd made it clear to her that no corner of this temple was off-limits to him and his warriors.

We'll see about that.

Jax strode back to the Flame Chapel, skirting the gallery at the back, before taking the door that led down to the infirmary. The High Priestess had also shown him around it—but today, he would check out the area on his own.

Yet when he reached the doors to the infirmary, they slid open to reveal two squat utility-droids barring the way. Behind them, a red-clad figure straightened, her gaze flicking his way. A second priestess lay upon one of the rows of neatly made beds in the long rectangular space. The patient's face was pale, and her companion was checking her vitals with a hand-held sensor.

"Access denied," one of the droids greeted him.

Jax glared at it, anger igniting in his gut. These two wouldn't be difficult to barge past—they were designed for service, not for defense. The sisters didn't have Mir-Ferrin battle-droids guarding their kitchens or infirmary.

However, knocking these two droids aside and forcing his way in wouldn't make him popular with anyone here.

Jax met the eye of the priestess who was tending the other. "Call off your droids," he barked.

The woman, around the same age as the High Priestess, tall and regal with tightly curled black hair, swallowed. She then shook her head.

"I can't, Captain. Lady Ava has left instructions that no Guardian of the Flame is permitted to enter here."

Jax folded his arms across his chest. "What if one of us requires medical assistance?"

The priestess held his eye. "Then you are to return to *The Star-Hawk* for treatment."

Fighting his rising temper, he shifted his attention to the wan-faced woman on the bed. She was in her mid-twenties and was watching him with wide eyes. "What's wrong with her?"

"A bad tonsil infection," the priestess replied. "Sister Margrit has a fever, so I'm keeping an eye on her."

Jax's gaze snapped back to her. "And who are you?"

"I'm Sister Thelia … I run the infirmary."

"Well, Thelia," he replied, letting a threat rumble through his voice. "For your own safety, I suggest you reconsider Lady Ava's instructions and allow me entry."

She lifted her chin, her gaze never wavering. They stared at each other for a few more moments before she replied, "No."

Jax's temper splintered.

"For fuck's sake," he growled. He then spun around, his cloak billowing behind him. Without another word, he marched away, heading toward the elevator that would take him up to the High Priestess's solar.

And as he walked, his anger simmered, molten in his gut.

The bitch.

Ava Mir-Brennan wasn't in charge here anymore—*he* was. And it was time she understood the new order of things.

8. PLAYING GAMES

LEAVING THE ELEVATOR, Jax strode across the wide landing and entered the library. The High Priestess's private solar was located at the far end.

Floor-to-ceiling shelves lined the library, crammed with leather-bound volumes. Protected by glass, these books told the history of the Sisters of Awe and the Gods, thousands of years written down in dusty tomes. During the tour Lady Ava had given Jax upon his arrival at the temple, she'd informed him that records had started long before the races of this sector took to the stars.

A handful of priestesses were studying in the library this morning, bent over ancient books, illuminated by lamps. They glanced up as Jax entered.

He ignored them, heading up the carpeted aisle between the tables, toward the gleaming wooden door of the High Priestess's office.

"Captain." One of the sisters stepped forward, moving as if to block his path. Jax recognized her: Sister Skylar, the High Priestess's Second. "You aren't permitted in there."

"Get out of my way," he growled.

Sister Skylar's eyes snapped wide. Nonetheless, she halted, letting him brush by.

Jax reached the office door, rapped twice to announce himself, and then threw open the door before entering the High Priestess's inner sanctum.

Aware of the shocked gazes of the sisters in the library, boring into his back, he kicked the door shut behind him.

His gaze then slipped past the austerely furnished office, zeroing in on the woman he'd come to face.

Dressed in close-fitting dark-red leggings and a tank top, the High Priestess sat with her back to him, cross-legged upon a dais before wide windows. She was seated in a meditation pose. At the sound of someone knocking on the door, she'd come out of her reverie and twisted, glancing over her shoulder.

"What the—" she began, her eyebrows crashing together.

"High Priestess," he barked, cutting her off. "You will not bar me access to anywhere in this temple. Is that clear?"

A beat followed, and then anger flared in her pewter eyes.

Satisfaction flickered up within him at the sight. The other Sisters of Awe appeared serene. But whenever she was around him, the High Priestess struggled to keep her temper.

Jax seemed to know exactly how to rile the woman—and now, he'd finally pushed her too far.

Good. He wasn't in the mood for being stone-walled. He wanted her pure, undiluted rage.

Swiveling around to face him, Lady Ava pushed herself up, rising to her feet. She then stalked, barefoot, down to meet him. Her appearance took him aback. He was used to seeing her in her flowing priestess robes. And even when they were training a short while ago, she'd been wearing a long ankle-length tunic.

However, the leggings and top she wore hugged the womanly curves of her body, emphasizing the magnificent swell of her breasts. A glittering obsidian pendant hung around her neck.

"How dare you?" she snarled, getting in his face. "This is my private space. You may not enter it without invitation."

"I'll go where I want," he growled back. Their faces were just inches apart now, and he could see the flecks of smoke and steel in her grey eyes. "That was the agreement."

"I didn't agree to it."

"The Wise Ones did … and that's good enough for me."

A nerve jumped in her cheek, revealing that although she didn't mind crossing him, the Wise Ones were another matter.

Pressing the advantage, Jax took a step toward her. "The clan leaders have given me complete authority here. Accept it." He was too close now, forcing her to retreat or their bodies would touch. Fury smoldered in her eyes though as she gave ground—one step after the other, until he'd backed her up against a wall.

Cornered, she glared up at him. "The kitchen, infirmary, and storage depots are out of bounds, Captain." She bit out the words. "The clan leaders have no jurisdiction here. Short of orders direct from the Wise Ones themselves, I will not give you or your warriors access."

Heat swept over Jax, his temper spiking once more. "Why not?" He leaned in close, placing one hand on the wall next to her head. "What are you hiding?"

He knew he'd gone too far but he couldn't stop himself. Something about this woman pushed his buttons. He felt the reins of control slipping through his fingers whenever they clashed, a sensation he didn't like at all.

Her brows drew together, even as her breasts rose and fell sharply now. He was standing so close that they were just an inch away from brushing his chest. "Nothing," she ground out.

"So, you're playing games with me, is that it?" If this woman wanted a fight, he'd give her one.

"No."

He lowered his head slightly so that his mouth hovered near her ear, before replying, "I think you are."

Moving so close was a mistake. He was seriously overstepping now, yet his temper had gotten the best of him. Standing so near Lady Ava made him acutely aware of her. They'd been close before, during training earlier, but this was different.

This time, he was suddenly noticing things he'd deliberately ignored before: the creamy texture of her skin, the fullness of her mouth, the delicious curves of her tall, strong body—and the scent of her skin. She'd used a body wash that smelled of peach, and he found himself dragging the smell deep into his lungs.

That was another mistake, for his gut tightened, lust igniting in his veins.

A second later, his groin answered, stiffening against the restrictive material of his body armor.

Jax started to sweat.

Shit. This was a complication he didn't need. He should step away, should distance himself, yet he didn't. He never backed down during an argument.

They stared at each other, and Jax marked the way her pupils dilated. Lady Ava's expression was stony, yet her eyes betrayed her.

She'd felt it too. This awareness, this pull between them.

The High Priestess was the first to shatter the moment. "If you have a problem with the limits I've imposed, Captain, then take it up with the Wise Ones." Her voice was steady, although it held a slight rasp.

"I shall," he rumbled. "I'll make sure there isn't a corner of this temple that's off-limits to me, *My Lady.*"

Lady Ava sucked in a deep breath. Her chest rose, the tips of those lush breasts, outlined by the close-fitting top she wore, grazing his chest.

Jax's own breathing caught as his cock started to throb.

Gods, what was wrong with him?

Her eyes narrowed. "You do that," she said, biting out each word.

"Oh, I will."

She exhaled sharply. "Get. Out. Of. My. Solar." Anger rippled off Lady Ava now; she enunciated each word like a curse.

Jax wondered then how much further he could push the High Priestess before she lost her temper. And what would she do if she did? Would she swear at him, shove him in the chest, slap his face, or try and knee him in the balls?

There was a part of him that wanted to find out—that wanted to drive this woman beyond her limits.

But this time, Jax didn't give in to his instincts. He knew what would happen if either of them lost their temper. From the moment he'd stepped out of his shuttle and laid eyes on this woman, they'd both been far too aware of each other.

It would take little for the tension between them to slide into something else.

He was straying into dangerous territory, so, this time, he let her have the last word—something he *never* did in an argument.

Drawing back, and trying to ignore his rock-hard, aching groin, Jax turned and walked away.

Ava walked through the temple with determination in her stride. On her way to the dining hall, she passed Guardians on patrol. They were *everywhere* these days. The warriors, clad in black and red, their faces partially hidden by their helmets, were an intimidating presence.

And after the incident the day before in her solar, word had spread around the temple that Captain Jax had barged into the High Priestess's inner sanctum to go head-to-head with her.

Lunch and supper following the altercation had been awkward. Not just because Ava refused to acknowledge the captain, but because her sisters watched them both with wide, worried gazes.

The looming threat had already made Ava's sisters nervous, and now they were upset. The High Priestess was to be obeyed in all things, yet this arrogant captain ignored her status. Ava had done her best to soothe their worries during the morning's service, although things wouldn't settle until she got Captain Jax on a leash.

Over the past day, she'd tried to think of ways to make her authority here clear. Sure, she'd ordered the captain from her solar, but not before he'd crossed the line.

He'd backed her up into a corner and stood so close that the heat of his body had wrapped itself around her like a cloak.

She'd been furious—she still was—but her breathing had become rapid, her heartbeat going wild at his nearness. And when he'd leaned in, his breath feathering across her ear, excitement had fluttered through her stomach, need pooling in her lower belly.

The Destroyer cut me down. She couldn't believe she'd wanted that asshole, yet she had. Her spacious solar had suddenly seemed cramped and airless with him present, and when she'd accidentally brushed her breasts against his chest, dizzying lust had crashed through her.

It was an awareness she intended to quash—along with him.

When she'd told Captain Jax he could go to the Wise Ones, she'd been bluffing. The last thing she wanted was for him to compromise her position here. She had to hope he wouldn't dare.

He'd arrived for breakfast before her, seated upon the dais at the end of the dining hall now as if he owned it. Captain Jax reclined in his chair, his obsidian gaze tracking her across the floor.

They'd already seen each other this morning, training just after the Fifth Chime. He'd taken her through sets of hand-to-hand combat drills, his manner businesslike and cool, before he'd set up a target on the far wall of the conservatory and shown her how to handle a laser-pistol.

The pair of them had spoken only when necessary, although all the while, Ava had silently fumed.

She had to find a way to put this male in his place—and later, while she'd been showering, she'd come up with an idea.

Sliding into her seat next to the captain, Ava cut him a sidelong glance. That was a mistake, for his dark gaze speared hers. "My Lady."

"Captain."

Utility-droids wheeled toward the dais then, bearing platters of flatbread and fruit.

Ava helped herself to some food and asked for a hot beverage before turning her attention back to Captain Jax once more.

"What time are you returning to *The Star-Hawk* this morning, Captain?"

"Directly after breakfast, My Lady."

She nodded. "Excellent. I shall be coming with you."

He inclined his head. "And why is that?"

"Since you want to oversee the supply drop-off, I'm interested to see what security measures your team employs that we don't," she replied, keeping her voice polite and emotionless.

He raised a dark eyebrow. "And what *are* your security measures, My Lady?"

Bristling at the thinly veiled insolence in his tone, Ava lifted her chin. "Supplies are delivered every thirty days. The freighter lands on the platform in front of the temple, and the entire inventory and unloading process is taken care of by droids. None of the priestesses interact with the pilot."

"And is all the cargo scanned?"

"Of course. The droids take care of it."

"You're using RD4 scanners, My Lady … they're old tech."

Ava scowled. "Maybe, but they haven't failed us yet."

His gaze narrowed. "Smugglers are lining their crates and holds with Villum these days … a material that only the latest scanners can detect," he answered. "We also scan the cargo ship before it enters the planet's atmosphere … that way, we ensure no danger gets anywhere near you."

The patronizing edge to his voice grated on her, yet she forced a polite smile. "Well then, I should like to observe these processes of yours, Captain. Maybe I can learn from them."

Did she imagine it, or did his jaw tighten?

Victory thrilled through Ava. Captain Jax didn't have a problem stomping around this temple and disrespecting its, and her own, boundaries. But he didn't like anyone doing the same to him. She was about to teach him a lesson.

Seconds passed before he gave a curt nod. "As you wish, Lady Ava."

9. THE DEAD SPOT

AVA FOLLOWED CAPTAIN Jax onto the shuttle.

Outside, a vicious wind whipped around the base of the temple, bringing with it stinging needles of grit. Dust devils had danced across their path on the landing platform as they walked across to the shuttle.

The captain made his way toward the front of the craft before taking a seat behind the pilot and co-pilot. The engines thrummed to life, causing the metal deck beneath Ava's feet to vibrate. Taking the empty seat next to Captain Jax, she reached for the safety harness and clipped it into place.

Meanwhile, a team of five warriors seated themselves.

The engine noise rose to a whine, and excitement curled in Ava's stomach.

This was the first time in fifteen years she'd left the surface of Pillarus One. For a long while, she'd gazed up at the sky, at the three moons that hung there, and fought the longing to travel amongst the stars once more. As a child, her parents had taken her all over the sector. A governor's daughter, she'd had the opportunity to visit many space stations and planets.

Yet she hadn't appreciated how lucky she'd been until she joined the Sisters of Awe. She wasn't going far today. Nonetheless, it was liberating to board a spaceship, to be able to get a taste of what she'd been missing all these years.

Her chest constricted then.

You shouldn't miss space travel, she told herself firmly. She shouldn't let excitement flutter up either. This journey should leave her unmoved. *This life is a privilege. It should be enough for you*.

But it wasn't, and she couldn't lie to herself. She often longed for more.

The shuttle lifted gracefully off the platform, swaying slightly as the wind buffeted it. Leaning forward, Ava peered out the cockpit window. The wind was bad today. However, there wasn't a hurricane predicted. As always, the sky glowed pink, although the wind had kicked up a lot of dust, turning the horizon hazy. Ava's attention then shifted to the spiky beehive carved into the mountain and the great tower that rose above it all.

Her brow furrowed. She hadn't seen the Wise Ones since they'd summoned her to them after Keisha's death and told her she was now High Priestess. She'd sent a couple of messages to them now, complaining about Captain Jax's behavior—but both missives had gone unanswered.

Nervousness fluttered up then. Had she angered them?

Keisha had met with them regularly, yet in the past months, they hadn't called for Ava, hadn't communicated with her. Surely, they would soon?

The shuttle rotated away from the temple before its nose lifted, and Ava was thrown back in her seat as the craft accelerated upward through the planet's atmosphere.

The journey was swift. One moment they were traveling through the dusty sky, the next, the curve of the planet glowed beneath them, contrasting against the dark depths of the void beyond. And there, orbiting the planet, was a ship. Golden and crab-shaped, *The Star-Hawk* was a light cruiser. Its color and shape were distinctive, marking it as a Mir-Brennan vessel—a gift from the Mir-Brennan clan-lady herself.

As they neared the cruiser, Ava glanced over at Captain Jax. He wasn't looking her way. Instead, his gaze was fixed ahead as he watched their approach. His expression was impassive.

Ava cleared her throat, drawing his gaze. "When will your reinforcements arrive, Captain?" she asked.

She was conflicted these days. The attack on Morvin had unsettled them all, and although Ava didn't welcome the presence of the Guardians of the Flame here, she had to admit that she'd feel safer with more cruisers orbiting Pillarus One.

"I don't know," he replied. "The clan leaders are still deciding on how many ships and warriors to provide us."

Ava frowned. "Is something wrong?"

He shook his head. "Just red tape. The Mir-Lelith clan-lord is reluctant to give any more assistance than strictly necessary. And now that the Mir-Brennans and the Mir-Ferrins have ended their feuding, he's nervous they might use the situation to create an alliance against him." His jaw tightened then. "We need more resources here … but the extremists will only become a bigger problem if the clan leaders don't get their shit together. They should be doing more than defending the Temple of the Gods … they need to hunt *The Creed* and put an end to them."

Ava eyed the captain. He had a blunt way of putting things, but she could still see his point. She wasn't going to openly agree with him though. The man's ego didn't need bolstering.

The shuttle angled toward the belly of *The Star-Hawk* then, as a hangar door slid open to admit it. Ahead, Ava spied a row of black and red uniformed officers waiting for them beside the docking station. They stood rigidly to attention as they readied themselves to welcome their captain back onboard.

"Commander, the *CS Frontier* has just come out of hyperspace."

"Thank you. Open a comm-channel."

Standing on the bridge of *The Star-Hawk*, Ava watched the lozenge-shaped silver freighter—a Mir-Lelith craft—cruising toward them. The *CS Frontier* had been delivering supplies to Pillarus One for the past five years. Mir-Lelith territory was the closest to this planet, and they'd never had any trouble with their suppliers.

But Captain Jax wasn't taking any risks, and although his obstinance irritated her, she also understood that these precautions were just part of his job.

Behind her, the female human officer Commander Asher had just spoken to put in an earpiece and touched the illuminated panel in front of them. As the woman informed the captain of the vessel of the new security procedure, Ava continued to watch the *CS Frontier*.

"Yes, Captain Jagar, we will need to sight *all* your papers," the officer replied. "Including your logbook."

A pause followed.

"Thank you, Captain," the officer said finally. "That all checks out. Please dock onboard our ship so we can inspect your vessel." Another brief pause followed then before the woman spoke once more. "That wasn't a request, Captain, but an order."

Turning from the wide bridge windows, Ava glanced over at where Commander Asher, a tall, lean man with hawkish features, stood next to Captain Jax. Both were frowning as they watched the officer speak to the cargo ship's pilot.

Eventually, the woman removed her earpiece and nodded to them. "He's not happy about it, but he's complying."

"Good," Commander Asher grunted.

Meanwhile, Captain Jax glanced over at Ava. "Does he usually have an attitude?"

Ava shrugged. She imagined Jagar Mir-Lelith muttering under his breath as he complied with the orders. Ava had only ever spoken with him via a comm channel once or twice—never face-to-face. She remembered he could be a little surly. "Jagar probably thinks you're being overly officious," she replied mildly.

Commander Asher's frown deepened at this, yet the captain's expression remained impassive.

Ava turned back to the bridge window to see the freighter closing in on them. Moments later, it disappeared into the belly of the cruiser below.

A silent wait followed on the bridge. Ava didn't speak to any of the officers around her, and they didn't bother to engage her in conversation either. Nonetheless, she was aware of the stares she'd drawn when she'd emerged from the shuttle behind Captain Jax earlier.

None of them expected the High Priestess of Awe to pay them a visit.

However, Ava ignored all the attention she was drawing. She was too fascinated by her immediate environment. The cruiser's bridge was all gleaming surfaces and flickering lights with wide windows on all sides.

Ava's attention shifted to where Pillarus One hung beneath them. From this position, she could clearly see the terminator—the corridor where life existed between the dark and light sides of the planet. Over the centuries, that corridor had tightened. One day, the planet would no longer be habitable; the order would have to move elsewhere.

However, that wouldn't be in Ava's lifetime.

"We've run our scans, Sir," one of the other officers eventually broke the silence. Ava turned to see a large Nandoon had swiveled on his chair to face his commander. "However, we've found a 'dead spot'."

Captain Jax pulled a face. "Sounds like he's got a smuggler's hold on board."

Ava tensed. "What?"

"They line them with Villum," Commander Asher replied, confirming what Captain Jax had told her that morning. "Most scanners can't detect any dead spots … but ours can." He turned back to the Nandoon. "Tell our security team to open the hold. Let's see if the *CS Frontier* is smuggling anything into the temple."

Ava stiffened. "I can assure you we don't order illegal goods, Commander."

"That remains to be seen, My Lady," Asher replied before he focused on where his officer was relaying his orders.

Clenching her hands at her sides, Ava drew in a deep breath. She glanced over at Captain Jax to find him watching her, his expression veiled. Did he think she handled contraband too?

Ava's lips parted as she readied herself to inform him that if Captain Jagar had a smuggler's hold onboard his ship, it was news to her.

However, she never spoke—for an explosion rocked *The Star-Hawk*.

The cruiser shuddered, the groan of rending metal thundering through it, and then the bridge listed sharply.

Ava lurched forward, hands flailing as she tried to grab onto something. Her fingers clutched at nothing but air though, and an instant later, she collided with the hard wall of Captain Jax's chest. He'd fallen against one of the consoles, and his muscular arms locked around her like a cage as claxons started to wail.

Commander Asher pushed himself up off the wall, cursing, as the cruiser righted itself. "Status report!" he bellowed.

"Docking Bay 45C has been destroyed, Sir," the female officer who'd initially contacted the freighter announced. Her slender fingers flew across the console. "A pyro-detonator was set off." Her voice tightened then. "Our entire security team and the *CS Frontier* are gone."

Still pinned against Captain Jax's armored chest, Ava gasped.

"Airlocks around the explosion zone are in place, Sir," the Nandoon officer cut in, the wattles on his neck quivering. "The damage has been contained."

Nonetheless, the claxons still blared around them.

Panic thrummed through Ava. Twisting in the captain's grip, she placed a hand on his chest and pushed. He took the hint and released her. But when Ava stepped back and raised her eyes to his face, his expression was thunderous.

Their gazes locked and held for a long moment.

"A pyro-detonator?" he growled.

A wave of nausea swept over Ava, and she swallowed hard. "I had nothing to do with this."

"I know that."

"I don't understand … Captain Jagar Mir-Lelith has worked for us for years."

"Not any longer."

Ava's pulse started to thud in her ears. "*The Creed* got to him?"

"It would seem that way."

"But how?"

"Maybe they made him an offer he couldn't refuse," Commander Asher replied. He stood over a console, checking the damage reports. The commander was rubbing his shoulder where he'd collided with the wall.

"Or he believes in their cause," Captain Jax replied.

Commander Asher's hawkish features tensed. "A suicide run?"

Captain Jax shrugged. "We'll never know … either way, he's just blown a hole in the side of this ship and killed our people."

Bile surged up Ava's throat, yet she choked it down. "How many personnel did you lose?"

"Eight, we think," the commander rasped.

Wrapping her arms about her torso, Ava drew in a deep, steadying breath, and then another. The shock of what had just happened, and what it meant, hit her then.

The threat was real. The Guardians' arrival was timely indeed, for *The Creed of Truth* was making its move now, daring to strike Pillarus One.

Ava wasn't safe.

None of them were.

10. NOT UNDER MY WATCH

STRAIGHTENING UP AS she struggled to recover her breath, Ava met Captain Jax's eye.

It had been a tough training session. He'd pushed her hard as she blocked punch after punch and sought to land a few strikes of her own—but she'd welcomed his aggressive approach.

The hard physical exertion helped rid Ava of the tension that had wound tight inside her, ever since the explosion onboard *The Star-Hawk* the day before.

Upon returning to the temple, Ava had informed her sisters about what happened. Skylar had wanted to speak to her alone, to hear in more detail about the incident, yet Ava had avoided her.

She hadn't wanted to think about it or talk about it.

But this morning, she forced herself to confront the subject. It was time.

"Captain," she panted. "Just to let you know, I've given you and your warriors access to all areas of the temple. From now on, you have clearance to carry out security checks in the kitchens, infirmary, and storage depots."

It was an effort to drag the words out, to humble herself before this man, but she forced herself. She was worried he might go to the Wise Ones following the attack, and she wouldn't blame him.

She'd thought the danger to this temple was still remote, but she'd been wrong.

If Captain Jagar had been willing to sacrifice his own life to harm them, there was no telling who else would turn against the order.

Her skin prickled. If that pyro-detonator had exploded in the kitchens or storage depot, it could have brought down the whole temple. *The Creed* would then have no doubt declared their 'victory' on the Shadownet, announcing that the temple where the Eight were revered equally had been destroyed.

Captain Jax nodded, and Ava braced herself for a smug, patronizing comment.

None came. Instead, he walked over to where two towels hung off a tree branch, picked them up, and carried them back to Ava, handing her one. "Thank you," he said finally.

Eyeing him, Ava wiped the sweat off her face and arms. Her robes were impractical to train in, so she'd donned the close-fitting red tunic and leggings she usually wore for meditation. Around her neck, her Amulet of the Gods gleamed darkly in the pink light filtering in through the conservatory windows.

"The Mir-Lelith clan-lord shouldn't deny you more warriors or ships now," she pointed out.

He snorted. "No."

Ava toweled off her arms. She was an exhausted mess, yet the man in front of her was hardly sweating. "Any updates on the *CS Frontier* or Captain Jagar?"

"No one's claimed responsibility for it," he replied. "Not yet, anyway."

Ava pulled a face. "*The Creed* likely doesn't want to be linked to a bungled attempt. It doesn't look good." She paused then, meeting his gaze once more. "It seems I owe you an apology, Captain."

He inclined his head, his obsidian gaze glinting, but didn't reply.

Feeling her cheeks warm, Ava cleared her throat. She then straightened her shoulders, eyeing him. "I'm not too proud to admit when I'm wrong," she said, even as a voice inside whispered to her that she was. "I underestimated the level of the threat, but I can assure you I won't be doing so again. From now on, you have my full cooperation."

He still didn't reply, and Ava's pulse quickened then, heat flushing over her.

Dammit, the man didn't make apologizing easy. His silence rattled her.

"Right," she said, choking back the urge to snarl at him. "Since we're done, for now, I'll bid you good morning. I've got to brief my sisters properly about what happened yesterday … I don't want to induce panic, but they should know how close the danger is." Towel gripped in hand, she turned and headed toward the doors leading out of the conservatory.

She'd almost reached them when he spoke. "I'm sorry too, My Lady."

Ava's step faltered, and she glanced over her shoulder. Was he mocking her?

His expression was serious though.

Reaching up, he then dragged a hand through his short black hair, leaving it in spiky disarray. "I'm not used to compromising."

Ava folded her arms across her chest. "Really?" she replied, unable to keep the sarcasm out of her voice. "I hadn't noticed."

He pulled a face. "Yeah, I've been aggressive."

Ava watched him warily. She appreciated the apology, although she still didn't trust him. Words were easy—she wanted to see if he actually meant them.

Nonetheless, this was the closest the pair of them had come to a truce.

"Well, we didn't get off to the best of starts," she admitted grudgingly. "Truth is, I hated you before you even turned up."

His mouth lifted at the corners. "That explains a lot."

"I was angry that no one consulted me about having you here." Ava cut her gaze away then. Holding his eye was too intense. "The clan leaders made their decision, and the Wise Ones agreed. My opinion wasn't required."

He moved closer to her, covering the floor in long strides.

Ava held her ground, although there was a part of her that wished to shift back, to keep her distance from him. Especially after what had happened in her solar.

What exactly *had* happened? She wasn't sure—although she didn't want to repeat it.

Fortunately, Captain Jax halted when he was around three feet from her. "Is that what they do?" he asked then. "Make decisions without consulting the High Priestess."

"Sometimes," she replied, daring to meet his eye again. "They're called 'The Wise Ones' for a reason, Captain ... they see things that the rest of us do not."

He nodded, his gaze searching. "But you're pissed off, nonetheless."

"I am ... especially when a newcomer barges his way into my temple and starts treating me like one of his subordinates."

"I was out of line."

Their gazes held before she cleared her throat. "Yes, you were."

His dark brows knitted together. "I could try telling you I did it for your own good, for your protection ... but that would be a lie. I took this job because I wanted to run my own show for once. I was angry when I discovered I was supposed to share power ... with you."

Ava raised an eyebrow. "So, you're ambitious?"

He huffed a soft laugh. "Yeah."

"You're a career soldier then ... no family, no children?"

"The military has been my life since I was sixteen." Captain Jax's mouth quirked. "No woman would put up with my assignments."

Ava snorted. "That's not all she wouldn't put up with."

The captain folded his muscular arms across his chest, eyeing her. "Point made, My Lady."

"Yes, well ... I'm glad we've cleared the air." Ava backed away from him. It was time to go—the man's proximity put her on edge. She didn't have the time to stand around talking to him anyway. Now that *The Creed* was breathing down her neck, she had to prepare her sisters for the coming storm.

He nodded, those black eyes glinting. "Me too."

Nodding back, Ava turned and walked briskly toward the doors.

Jax watched the High Priestess leave. Standing alone in the conservatory, he exhaled sharply.

Shit. He couldn't believe he'd apologized—that they both had. He'd also revealed a few things about himself he hadn't intended to. How was he supposed to establish control here now, after what he'd just admitted?

After returning to the planet, he'd told himself he would contact the Wise Ones. It galled him to do so—to admit he couldn't handle the High Priestess without their assistance—but enough was enough.

But he hadn't gotten in touch with them yet.

The events of the day before had clearly gotten to him. When the High Priestess had insisted on coming up to *The Star-Hawk* with him, he'd been angry. It was a routine inspection of the incoming freighter, yet he knew what she was doing.

She wanted to push his boundaries, just as he had hers.

Instead, when the captain of the *CS Frontier* had set off the pyro-detonator he'd hoped to use on the planet, rather than be caught and questioned, she'd realized just how close danger was.

And when Jax had caught her in his arms, holding her as the cruiser righted itself, a wave of fierce protectiveness had swept over him. At that moment, he'd have laid down his life to defend one aggravating human female.

Muttering a curse under his breath, Jax slung the towel he gripped around his neck and made for the doors. Their training session had been grueling, but it wasn't enough for him. He needed a workout that would leave him exhausted.

He'd run a few laps around the base of the temple. It was windy outside again today; perhaps the stinging dust and strong gusts that pummeled like angry fists would help him focus. He had to get his head straight again.

Now that the threat to this temple was growing, he couldn't let himself be distracted. When the additional ships, weapons, and warriors arrived, he needed to have a plan ready to utilize them.

Jax's brow furrowed then. He also needed to be more careful with Lady Ava—to remember who *he* was, and who *she* was. Letting his guard down around her was dangerous.

They wouldn't be having another conversation like that again—he'd make sure of it.

11. DEVELOPMENTS

Two months later …

THE HUMAN MALE, clad in flowing black robes, strode through the corridors of his ship. Crew members bowed their heads in reverence as he passed, their shaven scalps gleaming in the harsh overhead lights.

Father Cillan nodded to them. However, he didn't slow his gait to strike up a conversation with any acolyte.

The way of Wis was silence unless necessary. The Truth couldn't present itself with the constant intrusion of noisy thoughts and chatter.

Father Cillan had just emerged from hours of meditation. After such a deep connection with The Seer of Truth, he still felt distanced from mortals. One day, once he made Wis the sole Galactic God, and the clan leaders were brought down and all citizens of this sector bowed to The Seer of Truth, Cillan too would achieve what he longed for—power.

Excitement sparked deep in his gut at the thought.

It was his destiny.

The corridors of his battlecruiser, a lozenge-shaped Mir-Lelith ship he'd bought from pirates, were plain and stark, all dull-grey girders and panels. The austerity suited him.

Wis frowned upon adornment.

Reaching the bridge, the doors whispered open before him. Father Cillan walked into a rectangular space with huge windows lining three sides. The vacuum of space winked at him, while black-robed figures glanced up from where they stood at brightly lit consoles.

"Father Cillan." The human female standing nearest turned to him, clasping her hands together before her abdomen and bowing her head in respect. "I hope your meditation was fruitful?"

"Thank you, Sister Elia," he murmured. "It always is."
Picking up the hem of his robe he stepped up onto the
dais, where the horse-shoe-shaped bank of consoles
and control panels sat. "Any developments?"

"Our brothers and sisters on Caldoros have
confirmed that they have now successfully tunneled their
way under the capital," Sister Elia replied, lowering her
voice to match his soft tone. "They have discovered an
underground cavern, directly under the central plaza."

Father Cillian halted, allowing himself the faintest of
smiles. "That's welcome news, indeed. The Seer of
Truth be Praised."

"The Seer of Truth be Praised," his officers on the
bridge echoed.

Father Cillian's gaze swept over their faces, noting
the eagerness, the gleam of fervor in their eyes. These
were his old guard. They'd been with him from the
beginning—a decade earlier when he'd committed
himself to this cause. Humans, Vulkar, and Rendak, they
were all unquestioningly loyal, both to him and Wis.

They weren't the only ones dedicated to the cause,
for *The Creed* was split into many cells nestled within the
sector. However, like Cillan, they'd given up everything
to fight for Wis.

Like him, they'd stop at nothing to further the cause.
The Mir-Lelith clan-lord was currently in Cillan's sights.
He intended to topple all of the three most powerful clan
leaders from power, but Aran Mir-Lelith would go first.

"Everything is falling into place," he said softly,
moving across the dais to the captain's chair. There, he
folded his lanky body into it. "As I have foreseen."

"Once we widen the entrance tunnel, the cavern will
provide the space we need to bring in enough pyro-
detonators to blow the central business district sky-high,"
Brother Drac rumbled.

Father Cillan cast the Vulkar a thin smile. "Good." He
paused then, stretching out his long legs before him and
crossing them at the ankle. The tunneling under Ard,
Caldoros's capital city, had been a long-term project. He

was pleased to see the end was in sight. Once the excavation was complete, they'd be ready to lay their trap for the Mir-Lelith clan-lord. "But we still need to deal with the Temple of the Gods."

"If I may speak plainly, Father," Brother Drac said gruffly. It was difficult for the Vulkar to keep his voice low, for he was naturally aggressive, but he managed—just.

Cillan inclined his head. "Of course, Brother."

"Smuggling in a pyro-detonator on that cargo ship was always a long shot. We planned it before the clan leaders sent military aid to Pillarus One," the Vulkar growled. "Captain Jagar insisted they didn't have the tech to find the detonator … but he was wrong."

"He was," Cillan agreed.

Jagar Mir-Lelith had shown his loyalty by blowing himself and his freighter up. He would have taken a few personnel onboard *The Star-Hawk* with him too—but he'd still failed.

Cillan had been sore about the unsuccessful attack ever since and had focused his attention on the various other 'projects' he was progressing. However, the time had come to look to the Temple of the Gods once more; he'd known that for days now, and had been secretly working on a solution.

"We need to go back there, Father," Brother Drac growled. "And this time, our attack needs to be *focused*."

Cillan nodded. It was good to see that Brother Drac was thinking along the same lines as him. "Oh, we will, Brother," he said softly. "I've been in contact with a Mir-Straken droid specialist … and we're about to make a *significant* purchase." An expensive one too—this item had cost him over a million credits. It was just as well *The Creed* had wealthy backers. Cillan's mouth quirked then, noting the way Brother Drac's black eyes glinted with excitement, before he added, "That's right, Brother … the High Priestess of Awe's days are numbered."

A dust devil danced across the hillside, narrowly missing the first of the hoppers that raced down the slope.

Piloting one of the craft herself, Ava glanced up at the pink sky. She'd checked the weather before departing. No severe wind events were scheduled for the next few days. Even so, there was often a breeze upon Pillarus One.

Her mouth curved then, exhilaration surging through her veins.

Since becoming High Priestess, she didn't often get out of the confines of the temple; yet she loved speeding across the hills beyond it on a hopper. The needle-nosed craft was light and responsive.

Riding it made her feel free.

She'd been looking forward to today for a while now, even if she was nervous about leading the upcoming ceremony. It was her first time, and she didn't want to mess it up.

Yet the tightness in her belly couldn't cast a shadow over her buoyant mood.

Out of the corner of her eye, she caught a flash of red—a voluminous cloak streaming out behind a hopper.

Captain Jax had accelerated so he rode next to her.

Behind them sailed a transbarge, piloted by one of the Guardians of the Flame. The group of six priestesses who'd accompany Ava to the Sky Altar, for the Blood rite, were on-board. There were also a few outriders, warriors perched on gleaming silver hoppers.

Today was the most important event of the year for the Sisters of Awe: the pilgrimage to the Sky Altar. It was a journey they made once every three hundred days, one they'd always made without incident. Yet Captain Jax had insisted they have an escort.

Their gazes met then, for an instant, and Ava's smile widened.

Fortunately, her relationship with Captain Jax had improved hugely over the past weeks. If he'd been so authoritative upon his arrival, Ava would have fought him. However, when he'd announced his security plans for the trip, she'd merely nodded.

The captain knew what he was doing—and she'd let him do his job.

Over the past two months, she'd had to get used to a far heavier military presence upon Pillarus One anyway.

Four cruisers now orbited the planet, and the garrison on the surface had increased from twenty to one hundred. There were warriors everywhere, both male and female, and many of them now resided in the purpose-built barracks attached to the temple.

These days, only Captain Jax and his officers ate their meals in the dining hall, while the others used the mess hall in the barracks. Although the Guardians did their best to keep a low profile in and around the temple, the peace had been shattered. Whenever Ava glanced out of the window of her solar or bedchamber, she saw them patrolling the hills around the temple or standing watch—silent, grim sentinels in their black and red armor.

And she *did* feel safer with them there. Ever since the incident with the supply delivery, she'd been on edge— as had her sisters. They all continued their combat training without grumbling now, anxious to do what they could to protect the sacred flame and the temple that housed it.

Glancing at the captain once more, Ava saw that he'd shifted his attention away and was now scanning the horizon. The warrior was on the constant lookout for threats. She hadn't seen him properly relax once since his arrival.

Feeling her gaze upon him, Captain Jax looked her way. He then maneuvered his hopper a little closer. "I'd be happier if you were traveling with the others on the transbarge, My Lady," he said, raising his voice to be heard over the engines.

Ava snorted. Of course, not all the tension between them had eased. She still held her ground on a few things. And riding her own hopper today was one of them.

"I'm perfectly safe," she replied, careful not to let her irritation show. She then inclined her head. "Especially since you're sticking to me like cement."

His mouth compressed just a little, a sign she'd come to recognize over the past weeks. Her stubbornness frustrated him.

Ava and Captain Jax saw a lot of each other these days. She trained with him at the Fifth Chime every morning and had now graduated to handling a laser-blade and even a laser-staff. They took all their meals together and met for regular safety briefings in the evenings. Captain Jax was difficult to read, yet she spent so much time with the warrior that she'd learned his moods, his subtle expressions.

It hit Ava then that she'd changed of late. Despite her worries about *The Creed*, her restlessness, and the loneliness that went along with it, had lessened a little. For years, she'd felt trapped here, cut off—but Captain Jax's company had eased that suffocating sensation.

Heat washed over her. The realization flustered her; she wasn't sure what it meant.

"You will need to take your lead from me once the ritual is done, My Lady," Captain Jax spoke once more, shattering her reverie, "since we must make camp at the foot of the mountain." He paused then, and she imagined that under his visor his dark brows were drawing together. "You will be vulnerable overnight, away from the temple."

"I understand," Ava replied. And she did.

She'd made the trip to the Sky Altar many times over the years and had never been in danger, but things had changed. There had been no further incidents over the past weeks, yet that didn't mean *The Creed of Truth* wasn't planning another attack.

Of course, they were. It was only a matter of time.

Ava's stomach clenched then. Suddenly, she wished the Sky Altar wasn't such a distance from the temple.

She'd been busy of late, for in the days leading up to the Blood Rite, she'd conducted extra services, honoring each of the Eight in turn. And the night before leaving, she and her sisters had held an all-night prayer vigil in the chapel. In the past, a sleepless night wouldn't have bothered Ava—for she took care to keep her life in balance. Yet, worryingly, she was tired this morning.

"This didn't need to be such a lengthy trip, My Lady," the captain pointed out then. "I offered you use of my shuttle. We could have been there and back in hours."

Ava sighed, knowing that the noise of the wind and the hopper engines drowned out her irritation. "We've already discussed this," she huffed. "The slopes around Mount Gilith are too rocky ... you'd never find a place to land."

"We could have cleared a space."

Her brow furrowed, a little of the exasperation she'd once felt toward her protector resurfacing. "The mountain and the lands surrounding it are sacred, Captain. I won't have you blasting rocks out of the way so you can land your shuttle."

Captain Jax didn't reply although she sensed his quiet disapproval.

Letting her last words lie, Ava focused her attention on the wide valley stretching toward them. She then opened the throttle, and the hopper leaped forward, living up to its name.

12. PERFORMING THE BLOOD RITE

IT TOOK THEM a while to reach their destination.

Jax spied the craggy outline of Mount Gilith some distance away though; the lonely peak rose high against the rose-hued sky like some great sawn-off tooth thrusting up from a rough sea of rock-studded hills.

The collection of hoppers and the transbarge wove their way through the valleys and gorges that threaded across the landscape while a cool wind pushed against them.

It was a tiring journey, and Jax was relieved when Mount Gilith finally reared overhead, and they reached the place they would make camp later.

Drawing up his hopper and letting it settle on the ground, Jax cut the engine and climbed off. Senses alert and hand resting on the grip of his laser-pistol, he did a sweep of his surroundings.

There was nothing to alarm him, although he noted that the wind here was much colder than at the temple. They'd traveled far north although that shouldn't have made any difference to the temperature; instead, it was the fact that Mount Gilith stood just a couple of klicks from the edge of the dark side of the planet that had cooled the air so.

The transbarge rolled to a stop nearby and then lowered to the ground with a hiss. Moments later, the sisters who'd follow their High Priestess up the mountain disembarked. Jax noted how they glanced nervously around, as if they expected black-robed figures to leap out from behind boulders.

Their jumpiness didn't surprise Jax. With each passing day, the tension within the temple grew. They were all wondering what tack *The Creed* would try next—as was he.

Shifting their attention back to the reason they were here, the women formed a line before the path that zig-zagged upward. They then knelt and bent their heads in reverence.

Watching them, Jax realized that Lady Ava hadn't been exaggerating. The Sisters of Awe clearly considered this place 'close to the Gods'. He glanced over at where his warriors had parked their hoppers. They now waited for his command, ready for action.

"Captain." Jax turned to see Lady Ava approaching him.

She wore a flowing crimson cloak today, which fluttered out behind her as she walked. The wind buffeted against her, flattening Lady Ava's high-necked tunic dress against her body.

Jax couldn't help it. His gaze, masked by his helmet's visor, dropped to the outline of her full, pointed breasts. The chill had made her nipples harden against the material. Swallowing, he let his gaze drop lower to the dip of her waist and the flare of her hips. She walked with purposeful strides, the laser-blade she wore at her hip bouncing against her thigh as she moved.

It had initially been a challenge to convince Ava to wear a weapon. Once she had, Jax had suggested she opted for a laser-pistol, as they were easier to use. Surprisingly, she'd chosen a laser-blade.

In truth, the ease with which she'd taken to wielding a laser-blade had impressed him. She still had much to learn, although the High Priestess could now defend, block, and attack with relative ease. He pushed her hard in their training sessions, yet she didn't appear to mind. If anything, he sensed she enjoyed it.

Nonetheless, as she approached, the High Priestess cast a look around, assuring herself that they were indeed alone here.

"My Lady," he greeted her.

"We shall begin the climb now."

He nodded. They'd already agreed his warriors would make camp after the ascent to the Sky Altar and the Blood Rite had been carried out.

"I shall lead the way, with my sisters following," she continued, her grey eyes narrowing just a fraction as if she expected an argument. "You and your warriors must remain at the rear."

Jax tensed. She hadn't informed him of that when they'd met the day before to discuss this trip—and judging from the glint in her eyes, she'd known he wouldn't be happy about such an arrangement.

If they'd had this discussion two months ago, he'd have gone for the jugular, and things would have gotten ugly. But he hadn't gained the control he'd wanted, and he'd had to swallow defeat. Instead, he and the High Priestess now worked together as equals.

Jax hadn't thought he was capable of compromise—yet it seemed he was.

As such, he softened his response. "That isn't safe."

Lady Ava took a step forward, closing the gap between them. Her boldness made his pulse quicken just a fraction. This woman never backed down—something that both aggravated and excited him.

And yes, she did excite him.

He tried not to dwell on it, but the truth was that his compromise wasn't just because he respected the High Priestess. Jax was developing an obsession with her. He saw Lady Ava regularly, yet somehow it wasn't enough. In the evenings, he often sat in his bedchamber, staring out at the endless twilight, and finding himself wondering how the High Priestess spent *her* evenings once she retired. That was idiotic though, for letting his thoughts stray in such a direction meant he started imagining things he shouldn't. Forbidden things.

"I knew you wouldn't be happy about this," Lady Ava said, her voice lowering, "but tradition … and respect for the Gods … dictates that it must be this way. We offer the Gods prayers on the way up to the altar, and there can't be any obstruction."

Inhaling deeply, Jax forced a nod.

He didn't like it. He wanted to be at Lady Ava's side the whole way up the mountain, but he'd gotten to know the High Priestess well enough of late to understand when arguing with her would get him nowhere.

He took a step back, distancing himself from her, his gaze sweeping to where Vander approached.

"The warriors are all ready, Sir," Vander greeted him. "What are your orders?"

"We're following the priestesses up the mountain," Jax replied curtly. "Get ready to move out."

The climb up to the Sky Altar was always a tough one. Ava had made the journey countless times over the years, yet, as always, by the time she reached the halfway point, her calves and the back of her thighs burned, her chest heaved, and sweat trickled down between her shoulder blades.

The path was long and narrow, and it zigzagged up so sharply it was hard not to get vertigo when you chanced a look down at where you'd come from.

Far below, the parked hoppers and transbarge looked like children's toys.

The wind picked up further as they climbed too, making the journey even more strenuous. Nonetheless, Ava welcomed the air's bite. It helped cool her down.

Reaching a lookout three-quarters of the way up, she halted a moment, letting the wind dry the sweat on her brow. Behind her, the scuff of feet warned her that her companions had also stopped a moment.

Ava sucked in a deep breath and withdrew the Amulet of the Gods from underneath her tunic. The obsidian pendant was warm from her skin. She then held it up to the weak light of the dying sun, her eyes fluttering closed as she whispered a blessing. She'd offered many prayers and blessings on the way up, as was expected, preparing the Gods for the rites that would follow once they reached the Sky Altar.

She closed her eyes then, letting the wind eddy around her, before she glanced over her shoulder at those climbing the mountain behind her.

As she'd asked, Captain Jax and his warriors were following at a respectful distance. Wearing full armor, his blood-red cloak billowing from his broad shoulders, the captain was breathing hard from the climb as he flipped up his visor and tilted his head.

Then, his black gaze ensnared hers.

And for a heartbeat or two, they merely looked at each other.

It was the first time since leaving the temple that Ava had seen his eyes, and a reminder of why she was often more comfortable when he kept his visor lowered. Jax Mir-Lelith had a way of looking at her sometimes that made her feel as if she were standing before him naked.

The moment drew out, and Ava was aware that the pounding of her heart had *increased* during her pause, rather than decreased. Her chest suddenly felt tight, and a strange excitement fluttered low in her belly. Suddenly, it was as if the two of them were standing alone up here.

Swallowing, Ava turned away. Gods, she needed to pull herself together. She couldn't let herself be attracted to him. The Captain of the Guardians of the Flame was off-limits.

Jaw tightening, she powered up the next incline, ignoring the screaming muscles in the backs of her legs.

She wouldn't let herself want him. There, lay madness and self-destruction.

Such was Ava's determination to outrun her secret desires that the last stretch up to the Sky Altar was far faster than she'd anticipated.

Even so, she was winded when she reached it.

Panting, she walked out onto the wide circular platform and let her gaze travel across the vista below.

They were high up here—for Mount Gilith was the tallest mountain on this side of the terminator. It had taken them nearly three hours to climb it, and her legs shook from the effort.

Letting the wind cool her heated scalp, Ava viewed the sea of rugged, red-stained ridges and hills beneath them. She could see the edge of the terminator clearly from up here, for the dark side of the planet began just a couple of klicks from the foothills of the mountain.

A chill marched over her skin as she gazed at the shadowed landscape.

Once, those hills and valleys had been habitable. Once, this whole area had been verdant and green. Yet all that remained was this narrow strip of life between a frozen wasteland on one side and a scorching desert on the other.

The scuff of feet behind her drew Ava from her introspection, and she turned to find her sisters standing nearby.

Like her, their faces were flushed, and they were breathing hard.

A few yards behind, Captain Jax and his warriors looked on. The Guardians had formed a line, their armor gleaming in the twilight. They would observe the priestesses now yet wouldn't interfere in the ritual that would follow.

Nodding to her sisters, Ava withdrew the Amulet of the Flame from under her tunic once more so that it lay, exposed, upon her breast. She then, slowly, reverently, knelt at the center of the stone platform and turned her face to the sky. Holding the position, she waited while the priestesses took their positions around her.

Ava's pulse quickened, as did her breathing. Suddenly, all her self-doubt, all the things she struggled with in private, lifted. Nothing mattered in this sacred place—nothing except the Gods.

Long moments passed before Ava finally whispered, "Gods and Goddesses of the Galaxy, we honor you on this blessed day." She paused then before slowly reciting the names of the Eight. "Jidea, Mistress of Fortune. Wis, the Seer of Truth. Aura, Bringer of Prosperity. Fara, Lady of the Light. Nain, Mistress of Darkness. Syr, Lord of Mercy. Raul, the Destroyer, and

Miradia, Bringer of Fertility … you are all named and honored."

Ava began then naming some of the lesser Gods. It was a long, involved ritual, and she was careful not to mispronounce any of the many names, or to leave any Gods out. To do so would bring ill fortune upon mortals—something none of them needed right now.

Eventually, she concluded her naming and let silence fall across the platform once more.

The sharp wind tugged at her, yet she barely noticed its sting.

Since beginning the rite, she'd fallen into a peaceful, meditative state.

Slowly she drew a jeweled dagger from her belt. It hung next to the laser-blade she now carried. However, unlike the weapon Captain Jax had given her, this one was ancient. It had belonged to High Priestesses thousands of years earlier, before humans took to the stars. The blade was speckled with age, yet the jeweled hilt still gleamed.

Ava's belly clenched then, a little fear splintering her peace. This was the first time she'd ever carried out this rite. She'd watched Keisha perform it many times but had never been the one to wield the blade.

The thought of what she must do now made her feel a little sick.

Drawing in a deep breath, Ava held out her free hand, palm upward. And then, without hesitating for a moment longer—for if she did, she might lose her nerve—she sliced herself across the palm.

Pain lanced like fire across her hand, and she bit back a curse. Even so, she let out a hiss between clenched teeth. *Shit.* That hurt. She then closed her fingers over the wound, watching as her blood leaked through her fingers and dripped onto the star that had been engraved onto the center of the altar.

Ava's eyes fluttered shut, dizziness sweeping over her.

There, the ritual was done.

Head bowed, she tried to ignore the stinging pain in her palm. Seconds passed, and gradually, the vertigo faded. Ava raised her head and opened her eyes to see that the center of the star was now dark with her blood.

Elation thrummed through her, eclipsing the dizziness and pain. The Gods would be pleased.

Around her, she heard the other priestesses' murmured prayers. The wind shrieked across the Sky Altar now as if the Gods themselves were calling to them, whipping away their whispers.

For years, she'd watched her predecessor from afar. Keisha had made the rite look easy, yet it wasn't.

Using her uninjured hand, Ava pushed herself upward and rose to her feet. Yet as soon as she straightened up, her vision speckled and her ears started to ring. She staggered, falling to her knees once more.

Ava swayed and would have collapsed if a strong hand hadn't clamped around her arm, steadying her.

13. DON'T GO THERE

"LADY AVA," CAPTAIN Jax's voice rumbled in her ear. "Are you all right?"

Ava shook her head, even as she leaned into him for support. "I stood up too fast, that's all."

"Don't worry … I've got you."

She rose to her feet once more, slower this time, before glancing Captain Jax's way. Half his face was covered by the gleaming helmet, yet his jaw was set, his mouth compressed.

However, her protector waited until they'd walked off the platform before saying anything else.

"Let me see your hand."

Turning to face him, she gently extracted herself from his hold. Aware then that her sisters had risen to their feet and were observing them, Ava held out her hand, uncurling her fingers so he could see her palm.

Already, the cut had stopped bleeding. Nonetheless, it would need tending to.

"Did you really need to do that?" Captain Jax murmured. He kept his voice low as if he didn't wish anyone else to overhear him.

"Afraid so," Ava replied softly. "It's called 'the Blood Rite' for a reason … the High Priestess's blood must stain the altar to give an offering to the Gods." She paused then, her mouth curving into a rueful smile. "I'm just lucky I have this position in our time … centuries ago, the High Priestess died on this altar. Each cut her throat by her own hand. The Sisters of Awe had to refill the position every year."

Captain Jax flipped up his visor with his free hand, his gaze meeting hers. His face then twisted. "Barbaric."

Ava huffed a wry laugh. "It was seen as an honor at the time … however, after a while, the order realized they were running out of priestesses, so they scaled back the ceremony to a bit of blood-letting instead."

Spying Skylar approaching, Ava turned to her Second and waited while the priestess reached into a pouch strapped about her waist. Wordlessly, Skylar sprayed on some antiseptic and then deftly sealed the wound with a strip of plasti-skin.

Immediately, the burning pain upon Ava's palm stopped. Glancing Captain Jax's way, she flashed him a quick smile. "See, there's nothing to worry about."

His gaze narrowed in reply, letting her know he wasn't reassured.

Warmth suffused Ava's chest then. She knew he was just doing his job, yet there was something about his protectiveness over her that made her feel cherished.

Idiot, she chastised herself as she glanced away once more. *Don't read into things … he's paid to make sure you don't come to any harm.*

A chill rushed over her then. This was bad. The Gods help her, she was far too affected by this man; she couldn't let herself go there, or she'd soon be in serious trouble.

Drawing in a deep breath, she shifted her attention to the priestesses who stood in a semi-circle around her, awaiting instruction. They all wore solemn expressions, yet their gazes shone.

The Blood Rite kept the goodwill of the Gods and helped the universe maintain its delicate balance.

Ava favored them with a smile. "Come, Sisters … it's time to leave."

One by one, the party descended the mountain. Now that the Blood Rite was completed, Ava allowed Captain Jax to take charge. He and two others led the way while the rest of his warriors followed behind Ava and her priestesses.

The journey to the bottom was almost as tiring as the climb though, for the way was steep and the surface rough. They zig-zagged their way down, and by the time Ava reached the halfway point, her legs started to feel rubbery, and she deliberately slowed her pace to avoid stumbling.

Tripping wasn't a good idea up here. There was no handrail, and a tumble off the edge would prove fatal.

As she walked, Ava found herself peering down at the foothills below, scouring them for any sign of trouble. In the past, it was unthinkable that anyone would dare attack them in such a sacred place—but *The Creed of Truth* had already proved they had no respect for the Sisters of Awe.

Once they reached those foothills, the warriors would put up a circle of survival-domes for them to shelter in overnight. Ava couldn't wait to retreat into hers and rest her exhausted legs. The Blood Rite had taken a lot out of her, both emotionally and physically, and she just wanted to rest.

Eventually, the path grew less steep, and they began their descent down the final slope that would take them back to where the hoppers and transbarge were parked. Sharp boulders loomed overhead, shadowing the path. The wind, freezing now, barreled in between them.

Ava drew her cloak around her. She knew they were close to the dark side of the planet, yet she didn't remember the wind being this bone-chilling in the past. They'd all be using the heating in their survival-domes, otherwise, the cold would prevent them from sleeping.

Ava's gaze traveled forward then to where Captain Jax strode at the head of their party. He had armor to protect him, but she wondered if he felt the cold. There were times when she wondered if he was invincible. She'd never seen him tired or uncertain.

A screech cut through the air, yanking Ava's attention away from the captain. Just in time too, for a large white arachnid—twice her size—leaped onto the path before her, knocking the warrior walking in front of her aside.

The man grunted as he collided with a boulder.

Ava skidded to a halt, her heart lurching into her throat.

The Gods help them all, what was an ice-crawler doing out here? Since their arrival, they'd been looking out for *The Creed*, not for local threats.

She'd only ever seen these insects once before, when she'd gone in search of Keisha—and they'd fled when she turned up on her hopper.

This one wasn't so timid, and out in the twilight, its bloated, pulsating abdomen glittered with frost. The arachnid's eight legs, long and muscular, were almost translucent as if carved of ice, while its row of eyes gleamed like wet shards of rock.

The arachnid followed the warrior it had knocked into the boulder, grabbing him around the throat with one of its claws.

Without thinking, Ava drew the laser-blade at her hip, flicked the setting to 'kill' with her thumb, and ignited it. With a hiss, a slender white blade lit up the twilight.

She never got the chance to intervene though, for Captain Jax was there, his own laser-blade drawn.

He lunged for the ice-crawler, just as it flung out a clawed appendage in his direction. A flare of blue followed as he ignited the cyan-shield on his wrist-comm, a large transparent buffer that all the warriors were equipped with. The claw bounced off the shield, just short of slicing into Captain Jax's face.

At that moment, Skylar's shout echoed down the path.

Ava whirled around to see that another ice-crawler had sprung from behind a boulder. It had knocked Skylar, who'd been walking just a couple of yards behind Ava, off her feet, and leaped on top of her, pinning the priestess to the ground. The cries of the five other sisters following close behind rent the air, yet Ava was only focused on Skylar.

She rushed at the ice-crawler, even as its head lowered and its jaws opened revealing long, pin-like teeth.

Skylar's panicked scream followed. She was struggling violently now yet was pinned under the ice-crawler's weight.

Nain curse it, the crawler was going to sink its fangs into Skylar.

With a shout, Ava leaped forward and drove the laser blade into the arachnid's abdomen.

In an instant, the ice-crawler sprang off Skylar, its long legs flailing before it rolled away.

Wheezing, it regained its footing and spun around.

And then that unnerving row of eyes fixed upon Ava.

For a second, they merely stared at each other—and then the beast charged. The injury Ava had dealt it must have been serious, yet it appeared unaffected as it scuttled toward her.

Ava went side-on, as Captain Jax had taught her, and met the crawler as it rose up, front claws swiping like knives. A sting of pain bloomed across one cheek as she struck with her laser-blade, but she held her ground.

The shimmering white blade cut through the ice-crawler's neck easily, meeting no resistance. And when the laser-blade came out the other side, the arachnid froze for an instant, its row of eyes bulging.

Ava held herself at the ready, preparing to strike once more.

There was no need, for the ice-crawler crumpled, its head rolling off its thorax.

Breathing hard, Ava stared at the corpse as if expecting it to miraculously reanimate and lunge at her. It didn't.

She then moved to Skylar, helping her up. Her friend's face was taut, her eyes wide, and she was shaking. Ava put an arm around her shoulders as they turned to see what had befallen the first of the ice-crawlers that had attacked their party.

It too was dead—cloven in half by a laser-blade. The arachnid's abdomen steamed in the cold air, emitting a foul, sulfurous gas.

Captain Jax stood over it, while the warrior the ice-crawler had attacked had just peeled himself off the boulder and was rubbing his neck. Meanwhile, the captain and another, female, warrior who'd been leading the party were scanning the area, ready for another attack.

Ava's racing pulse kicked up a notch as she glanced around her. How many more of those crawlers were nearby? When she looked behind her, she saw that the rest of the security team had mobilized, positioning themselves around the remaining priestesses, laser-pistols raised.

Ava's sisters had also drawn the laser-pistols and laser-blades they carried. They looked nervous—as none of them had actually used their weapons in combat before. And of course, they were standing on sacred ground. They weren't supposed to wield arms here.

But, in contrast, concern about offending the Gods had been the last thing on Ava's mind—when the ice-crawler had attacked Skylar, there had been no time for hesitation.

Seconds passed, and then Captain Jax moved around the corpse of the ice-crawler he'd slain, approaching Ava in long strides. His visor was up, and his gaze never left her face.

Likewise, Ava didn't break his stare.

"That was impressive, My Lady," he said, drawing up before her.

Ava smiled, even if her legs were now trembling badly—a result of fatigue and shock. "I had a good teacher."

"You kept your nerve."

She swallowed. "I wasn't going to let it kill Sister Skylar."

He stepped closer then, removing one of his gloves. And then, under full view of everyone present, he reached out with his hand, using his thumb to gently wipe the blood upon her cheek. "It caught you here."

Ava stopped breathing. His touch set every nerve ending in her body alight. "Is it deep?" she whispered.

"No, just a scratch … you were lucky." He moved nearer still, and Ava forgot they weren't alone and that all his warriors and her sisters were watching their exchange. "You took a risk."

Ava didn't break his stare. "I did … and I'd do it again to save one of my sisters."

Jax stared down at the High Priestess. In the aftermath of the attack, her cheeks were flushed, and she was still breathing hard.

Her grey eyes glinted as she held his gaze—and Jax's body responded. His stomach clenched, lust barreling into him. A moment later, he started to sweat.

Gods, he had to rein it in.

What he wanted to do was haul this woman into his arms and savage her mouth with his. However, with his warriors and her sisters looking on, and the fact Ava Mir-Brennan was seriously off-limits, it would be a moronic idea.

But for a few seconds, he almost forgot the oath he'd sworn upon taking this job. Instead, his gaze dropped to her tantalizingly full lips, and he wondered what she'd taste like. And if they'd been alone, how she'd respond if he kissed her.

Don't go there.

His gaze snapped up, meeting hers once more, and he forced himself to nod. "Have ice-crawlers ever bothered you here before?"

"No." The High Priestess swallowed before glancing over at the motionless insect beside her. "They've been known to venture out onto the shadowlands between the dark side and the habitable zone … but not this far in."

"The wind's never been this cold at Mount Gilith," Sister Skylar spoke up then, her voice husky. "I think that's why they were able to travel this far from the dark side."

Jax's attention shifted to the priestess. Standing at Lady Ava's side, the woman wore a haunted expression. Of course, she'd had a shock and had nearly felt the bite of the ice-crawler's fangs. Nonetheless, her explanation sounded plausible.

"The terminator is narrowing," Lady Ava added. "As the sun dies, so does this planet."

Jax frowned. "But surely, the end is still a long way off?"

The High Priestess sighed. "It is … but in the meantime, the strip of habitable land gets narrower and narrower."

"Mount Gilith may not remain safe to visit," he pointed out. Secretly, he was annoyed that he hadn't taken the ice-crawlers more seriously—he'd been too focused on *The Creed*.

"Perhaps … one day," Lady Ava replied, her jaw setting in that stubborn way he'd come to recognize. "But until the base of the mountain is carpeted with ice-crawlers, we shall make the journey."

Their gazes fused once more and held.

Jax was tempted to argue with her. Yet he checked himself. It wouldn't help the situation, and they were exposed out here. Despite that his warriors had secured the area, Jax didn't want to take any risks. Instead, he'd ensure the High Priestess was safely inside a survival-dome with members of his team on guard.

That being the case, he merely inclined his head and stepped back, wisely widening the gap between them once more.

14. AT ARM'S LENGTH

"I SHOULD TAKE a look at your cheek."

Ava glanced up from unfastening her cloak to see that Skylar had ducked into the dome. Her Second had looked deeply shaken after the attack, but ever since they'd made camp, she'd recovered quickly. "It's all right," Ava replied with a smile. "You heard the captain earlier. It's just a scratch."

A groove appeared between Skylar's eyebrows. "Even so, ice-crawlers carry bacteria on their claws. I'd better disinfect it."

With a sigh, Ava submitted, waiting while Skylar dug into the pouch at her hip and produced her antiseptic spray. Around them, the smooth rounded sides of the survival-dome arched overhead. The makeshift shelters were easy to put up—at the press of a button, a flat circular disc expanded into a dome large enough to shelter at least two.

Stepping close, Skylar tended to the scratch, her gaze narrowing a little as she inspected it. Then, stepping back, she nodded. Ava's Second was one of the five priestesses within the temple who'd been medically trained. As such, she did shifts in the infirmary along with Sister Thelia.

Skylar's gaze met hers then, her expression veiling. "Captain Jax seems to take a special interest in you, Ava," she observed softly.

Heat flushed over Ava. Skylar's comment threw her, although she should have expected this.

"No, he doesn't," she replied with a snort, hoping her embarrassment hadn't made her blush. "You know he's been my shadow ever since he arrived on Pillarus One. I can't get rid of the guy."

Skylar cocked an eyebrow. "The looks he gives you could melt Lazda Steel," she murmured. "Be careful."

Ava's heart started to pound. Gods, her Second had picked up on the subtext between her and Captain Jax earlier. For a few moments there, they'd both forgotten where they were. *Who* they were.

Skylar had just reminded her of the situation. She was supposed to be setting an example, not staring inappropriately at the head of her security team. Nonetheless, she wasn't going to admit such to her Second. The last thing she needed was for any of her sisters to lose faith in her.

She had to brazen this out.

"There's no need to worry, Skylar," she assured her friend. "I think you misinterpret the looks Captain Jax gives me." She pulled a face. "Half the time, I'm sure he wishes he could strangle me."

Skylar nodded, even if her gaze was still watchful. "I don't think he's ever had a woman stand up to him before."

Ava's mouth quirked. "And I don't intend to stop. However, I think he understands now that we both want the same thing. I appreciate everything he and his team are doing to protect us." She paused then, sobering. "When *The Creed* comes for us … we all need to be working together."

"Maybe," Skylar answered, a note of censure in her voice now. "Just not *too* closely."

Ava and Captain Jax didn't speak on the journey back to the temple.

It was easy enough to avoid conversation. The whine of the hoppers was loud, as was the whistling wind, and Captain Jax wasn't the chatty sort. Like Ava, he didn't try to initiate conversation.

All the same, she was aware of his presence, riding just a couple of yards to her right.

She didn't look his way, but that didn't mean she could ignore him.

Jax Mir-Lelith wasn't someone easily ignored.

Hours earlier, after Skylar had left her survival-dome, Ava had stretched out onto her sleep-mat.

Be careful. Her Second's warning rang in her ears for a long while.

Ava's chest had grown tight, heat sweeping over her.

Dammit, things were getting out of control. The attraction between her and Captain Jax seemed to have a life of its own—and whenever they were near, it buzzed like an ignited laser-blade. She wasn't surprised Skylar had noticed; she just hoped her other sisters hadn't.

And now Ava was conflicted. She and the captain worked well together, and their cooperation was essential for the protection of the temple.

But things couldn't continue as they had.

If they did, the inevitable would happen.

Even now, seated astride her hopper, gaze fixed upon the horizon, Ava fought the desire that drew her in like a tractor beam.

No, she couldn't go there.

She had to center herself, to find a place of calm. As soon as they returned to the temple, she'd go to her solar and meditate for a few hours. She needed to focus. Protecting this temple was important, but the Gods were paramount. Ava was their mortal conduit. She had to keep her mind unsullied.

You must step back from him.

Heat prickled her skin once more. As much as she didn't want to admit the truth, she couldn't shy away from it. Without realizing it, she'd gone from hating Captain Jax to developing a crush of sorts on him. The change had crept up on her, yet now she faced it, panic clawed its way up.

Be careful.

Wise advice, and she'd take it.

A sickly sensation washed over Ava then. *Gods, what if it's too late?* Her attraction to Captain Jax was seriously starting to affect her. She might not have acted on her forbidden desires, but, like it or not, she *was* compromised.

When they returned to the temple, she had to not only keep Captain Jax at arm's length, she had to find a way to erase him from her thoughts.

No, she wouldn't ruin everything she'd worked so hard for. Somehow, she needed to fix this.

"I think it's time I started training with the other priestesses."

Lady Ava's words, which came toward the end of a largely silent supper, made Jax glance up.

Her tone was light, yet she wasn't looking his way.

Jax's gaze narrowed a fraction.

Something was wrong. He'd sensed it ever since they'd pulled up in front of the temple a few hours earlier.

The High Priestess's manner had been polite yet cool whenever she addressed him. And she refused to look him square in the eye as she usually did. Without a backward glance, she'd then imperiously swept into the temple, her cloak billowing behind her.

At the time, he'd dismissed her manner because of fatigue and stress—the pilgrimage to Mount Gilith hadn't gone as planned, and she'd nearly lost one of her priestesses.

However, she was still behaving strangely.

"Why is that?" he asked calmly, digging his spoon into the mushy root vegetable stew before him. Over two months since his arrival, and the food here hadn't gotten any more palatable.

Her steel-grey gaze flicked his way briefly before returning to her meal. "I'm comfortable to do so now … and I think they'd appreciate it."

"Would they? I thought you didn't consider it 'proper'?"

"I didn't," she replied, shooting him a glance then. "But not anymore. It would create a greater sense of unity within the temple if my sisters saw me training alongside them."

"I wasn't aware unity was lacking."

Lady Ava reached for her glass of water and took a sip. "They've had a lot of upheaval of late … and with each passing day, we all worry what *The Creed* is plotting. My sisters need me."

"It's your choice, My Lady." And it was. He wasn't going to insist she continue training alone with him if she didn't want to.

"Thank you." She took another sip of water before carefully placing it on the table.

Was Jax imagining it, or was there a slight tremble in her hand?

Lady Ava was hiding it well, yet she was nervous. Something *was* up with her.

Below the dais, the priestesses seated at the rows of tables were finishing their meals, as were his warriors. Soon, they'd all file from the hall and return to their duties.

"We're due a briefing session this evening, Lady Ava," Jax reminded the High Priestess then. "I want to go over a few security lapses I've noted of late."

She turned to Jax then, giving him her full attention. "Security lapses?"

"Yes, some of your priestesses aren't being careful enough." Before leaving for the Blood Rite, he'd caught one of them, a flighty young novice named Sister Yinna, coming inside from taking a stroll outside, unarmed. "Shall we meet in your solar, as usual?"

Lady Ava huffed a sigh before reaching up and massaging her temples. "Can we postpone it until tomorrow, Captain? I have a headache."

He frowned. "Are you feeling all right, My Lady?"

"Not really." She made a face, cutting her gaze away from his once more. "But I will after a decent rest."

"I'm going to have to postpone our briefing again, Captain."

Jax was striding toward Lady Ava, intending to ask her what time they were to meet. But she anticipated him.

They were in the atrium near the main doors to the temple. It was the evening after their return from the Blood Rite; supper had come and gone, and with the wind rising to hurricane force outdoors, the great Lazda Steel doors had rumbled closed, sealing them all inside.

Lady Ava had just finished a patrol of the lower levels of the temple, something she always did after supper. Jax caught her just before she went upstairs to begin her evening meditation.

Already the wind had risen to a steady whine, clawing at the metal. It was the third hurricane to hit since Jax's arrival on this planet, although he'd yet to get used to them.

Halting before the High Priestess, he didn't bother to mask his frown. "And what's the reason this evening, My Lady?"

His voice must have betrayed him too, for a groove appeared between her eyebrows. "It is my eve of prayer at the altar … once I complete my meditation, I'll spend the rest of the night in the chapel."

Jax's mouth pursed. Well, she had him there. The High Priestess's eves of prayer were unnegotiable, an essential part of her role. There wasn't any point in questioning it. However, she wasn't going to get out of meeting with him.

"We'll speak tomorrow then," he said firmly. "As I said, some of your priestesses need disciplining. Sister Yinna and Sister Luna have both stopped carrying weapons. And Sister Thelia has started skipping combat training in the mornings. They're getting complacent."

Lady Ava stiffened at this news. They both knew that some of her sisters had always struggled with the idea of carrying weapons, just as much as their High Priestess had. "I'll talk to them."

"Good ... but that's not the only thing I want to discuss. I'm designing a new security plan for the temple ... and for the perimeter around it. I want to go over my ideas with you."

Interest sparked in her eyes—but a second later, her gaze veiled. "Sister Skylar will be happy to discuss all of that with you," she replied briskly. "I've given her the authority."

And with that, Lady Ava turned and walked off.

Jax watched her go, his frown slipping into a scowl.

What was her problem?

Jax waited until the last of the three novices filed out of the library before stepping inside. As expected, Lady Ava was putting away the books she'd been studying with them.

"Good morning, My Lady," he greeted her brusquely.

The High Priestess glanced up, her statuesque frame going rigid. "Captain."

"You weren't at breakfast this morning," he said, closing the gap between them in long strides.

She shrugged. "I was tired after training."

It was a weak lie, but he didn't call her on it. Jax stopped before the High Priestess, deliberately boxing her in between the wall and cabinet. If she wanted to escape, she'd have to shove him out of the way. "I want to have a word."

"I'm busy, Captain."

"You're always busy." It was true. She'd successfully avoided him for days now, but he wasn't letting her do so any longer. "But I'm sure you can spare ten minutes now. I checked your schedule. You're not due to go down to the chapel yet."

Her mouth pursed. "We don't have anything to talk about, Captain. I trust you know how to do your job … and don't need to be kept informed of every move your team makes. I thought Sister Skylar was keeping you updated about the daily business within the temple?"

Anger sparked deep within Jax, although he suppressed it. He wasn't going to let this woman get to him. "She does, but *we* agreed to work together, Lady Ava."

She met his gaze squarely. "And we still are. I'm not obstructing you in any way, am I?"

Silence fell between them before Jax eventually asked, "Have you got a problem with me, My Lady?"

She arched an eyebrow, although he caught the way a nerve flickered under one eye. "No … not these days, anyway."

"Ever since we returned from Mount Gilith, you have been avoiding me." Jax folded his arms across his chest. "Why?"

Lady Ava stared back at him for a moment, and then, to his surprise, she growled a curse under her breath before muttering, "You always have to push things, don't you?"

He nodded. It was his way. "Answer the question."

"All right," she snapped, her grey eyes glinting. "I don't think the relationship that has developed between us is seemly."

His jaw snapped tight. "*Seemly*?"

"Yes … proper."

He scowled. "I know what 'seemly' means, My Lady."

She raised her chin, her gaze narrowing. "As the High Priestess of Awe, I must set an example to my sisters. You and I have been spending too much time together." She swallowed then, revealing that underneath her anger, his proximity was making her nervous. "It has to stop."

15. YOU KNOW

AVA OPENED HER eyes, slowly coming out of a deep meditative state.

Learning to meditate hadn't come easy to her. She had a busy mind, and it had taken Keisha a long while to train her how to quiet it. Nonetheless, a High Priestess had to learn how to master her thoughts.

Especially when her thoughts seemed to have a mind of their own.

Ever since returning from the Blood Rite, there was a part of Ava that rebelled against the new stance she'd taken toward Captain Jax. But her will was stronger.

Their argument earlier in the day had been awkward, but now that she'd spelled things out to him, he'd back down.

He'd leave her alone.

Ava's chest tightened, a hollow sensation filtering through her.

Ever since she'd started spending more time with Captain Jax, her loneliness had eased. However, now it would return, along with the restlessness that sometimes made her want to crawl out of her skin.

But she would handle both sensations, as she always had, with meditation and prayer.

Sighing, Ava pushed herself up off the cushion she sat cross-legged upon to meditate.

She'd taken the right path, the sane one. She'd get through this—she had to.

Nonetheless, even an hour's deep meditation hadn't been able to soothe her.

Dammit, she'd waited too late to back off from Captain Jax. The damage had already been done—over two months of working closely, of training together, had given her a taste of something she could never have.

"Too bad, Ava," she muttered, stepping down off the dais. "This is the life you chose … this is what you wanted."

They were tough words, but something inside her still rebelled.

The heavy steel shutters surrounding the solar groaned then, rattling as the hurricane outdoors battered the temple with all its might. It had been raging for two days now. Most evenings, Ava would mediate before a vista of jagged red-stained mountains and a pink sky, with one of the moons, usually Janessa, hanging overhead.

But this evening, it sounded as if wild beasts were trying to tear their way into the temple. The howling wind and the shuddering of the walls and windows put Ava's already taut nerves further on edge.

It was getting late—time for bed. Slipping on the light slippers she often wore in the evenings, Ava left the solar, padding through into the library beyond. She was still dressed in the clothes she wore for her stretching routine and meditation— leggings, and a sleeveless tunic, with the Amulet of the Gods around her neck. During busier times of day, she'd always change back into her formal attire and fasten a cloak around her shoulders, for it was important to set an example to the other priestesses. This evening, she didn't bother.

But instead of retiring to her quarters, Ava lingered in the library. Walking the aisles between ancient volumes protected behind glass, she reached a cabinet at the far end. She lowered her face so that the security panel could take a retinal scan and waited for the lock to disengage. Only the High Priestess had access to this cabinet and the priceless, ancient book inside it.

Opening the door, she gingerly picked the book up.

It was heavy, bound in leather that was worn and cracked by the ages, and filled with yellowing pages made of thin parchment.

Ava carried it over to one of the reading desks and carefully put the book down, switching on a reading lamp above her head. Then, she traced her fingers over the embossed leather cover, marveling at the age of this volume.

Although she knew she was allowed to touch it, she had refrained from doing so—waiting until she needed to remember just how important her role was, and the responsibility that had been passed down through the ages. This evening, she did.

This book documented the chaos that had once reigned in the galaxy before its citizens turned to the Gods for guidance. It was a reminder, not that she needed one, of how dangerous *The Creed of Truth* was. The extremists wanted anarchy, and if they ever got their hands on this volume, they'd incinerate it.

Peace had always been hard-won in the Rith Sector, and in hard times its many sentient beings looked to the Gods—which was why this temple and everything in it had to be kept safe.

Hardly daring to breathe, she opened the book, wincing at the way its spine creaked, and turned to the first section. She began to read and within minutes was lost. Pulling up a stool, she immersed herself in another time and another place.

Ava wasn't sure how long she sat there reading.

Nonetheless, she was so lost in the book that she didn't hear the whoosh of the library doors opening. It was only when the thud of approaching booted footsteps reached her that she looked up.

Captain Jax was walking toward her. Dressed in a black body suit, he covered the yards between them fast as he had earlier in the day in the library. His brow was furrowed, his expression grim. As always, a laser-blade hung from his left hip, and laser-pistol from the right.

Jolting out of her reverie, Ava straightened up.

What was *he* doing here? Hadn't she made herself clear earlier?

"Captain," she snapped. "Is something wrong?"

He halted a few yards away. "Your droid alerted me that you didn't return to your quarters, My Lady."

Ava frowned. What was Dee Dee doing contacting Captain Jax over something so minor? "That was hardly necessary," she replied with a snort. "I was only staying up a little late reading."

He raised a dark eyebrow. "It's now not long before the Third Chime, Lady Ava."

Tensing, Ava glanced down at her wrist. She'd taken off her wrist-comm to meditate and hadn't replaced it, leaving it inside her solar. She hadn't realized so much time had passed, and without the wrist-comm, her droid wouldn't have been able to contact her. "Shit," she murmured. "I lost track of time."

Captain Jax moved then, walking up to her shoulder so he could see what she was reading. "The book's good, I take it?"

"It is," she replied, stifling a yawn. Now that she knew it was the early hours of the morning, she suddenly felt tired.

"It looks very old … and fragile."

Ava glanced up at his face to see his gaze tracing the lines of slanted handwriting. "That's because it was produced over five thousand years ago."

"I don't recognize the language."

"You won't … it's long dead. However, all the Sisters of Awe learn it so we can read the ancient books."

"And what's this one about?"

Ava tensed. They shouldn't be in here alone like this. After the words they'd exchanged earlier, she knew it and so did he. However, she was too tired to keep her guard up. Surely, it wouldn't hurt to tell him about this book?

"It tells of how we came to believe in the Galactic Gods … and how things were before."

The captain's head inclined. "And how *were* things?"

She flashed him an arch look. "So many questions tonight, Captain. Do you really want to know, or are you just being polite?"

Captain Jax's gaze held hers. "I never say anything I don't mean, My Lady."

Ava's pulse quickened at the rough timbre of his voice. She then cleared her throat. "The galaxy was a mess in the past," she admitted with a sigh. "I'd known the origins of this order rose from the ashes of anarchy … but I hadn't realized just how bad things were."

The captain's brow furrowed. "For example?"

"Whole systems were at war with each other … clans were torn apart … and pirates ruled the shipping lanes. The Rith was one of the most lawless, dangerous sectors in the galaxy."

"And the rise of the Galactic Gods put an end to all of that?" Ava heard the skepticism in the captain's voice. It didn't surprise her. Although he revered the Gods, he was a pragmatic man, a soldier.

"They gave the citizens of this sector common ground," she replied after a pause. "Something to value besides their petty squabbles. It took a while, but with the passing of the decades, order settled."

"The Galactic Gods might have brought stability … but faith doesn't fix everything," Captain Jax pointed out with a rueful shake of his head. "If it did, the Mir-Brennans, the Mir-Leliths, and the Mir-Ferrins wouldn't have been at each other's throats for the years."

Ava released another sigh. "No," she agreed softly. "But at least they've made peace now … and believe me" —she gestured to the book before her— "things were *much* worse before."

"*The Creed* accuses the clan leaders of thinking they're above the Gods," Captain Jax said, meeting her eye once more. "Do you agree?"

Ava tensed. It was a deliberately provocative question. "It's true that over the years the clan leaders have followed their own agendas rathering than respecting the will of the Eight," she answered cautiously. "But, unfortunately, power corrupts." She paused then, shrugging. "That said … they hired you and your team to protect us."

His mouth lifted at the corners. "They did."

Ava inclined her head. "And what about you, Captain? Do you think the clan leaders have our best interests at heart?"

"Not really," he murmured. "I believe *all* of us are just looking out for ourselves … no religion will ever change that."

Their gazes held for a few moments before heat rolled over Ava. Gods, his directness cut like a laser-blade through her defenses. She'd missed talking to him, missed the way he spoke straight from the gut.

She'd never met anyone like Jax Mir-Lelith.

Suddenly, it felt overly hot and airless in here. It was time to stop this conversation before it got them into trouble.

She gently closed the book and picked it up, rising from her stool. "I'd better get some rest," she murmured. "And I apologize for Dee Dee waking you up. The droid can get a bit overprotective sometimes." Walking over to the cabinet, she carefully replaced the book.

"Your droid didn't wake me up," Captain Jax replied from behind her. "I don't sleep well these days, anyway."

Ava pushed the cabinet door closed, listening as the lock clicked, before glancing over her shoulder. "You should visit the infirmary. Sister Thelia will give you something to help with that." Her voice died away when she saw the look on his face. His expression was strained, even as his gaze burned into her. Ava stilled. "What's wrong?"

"I don't think Sister Thelia has anything that could cure what's wrong with me … Ava," he said roughly.

Her breathing caught. He'd never called her by her first name before. It was far too intimate, and yet at the same time, it thrilled her.

They stared at each other, the air between them shivering with tension before Ava wet her suddenly parched lips. "What's the matter with you?"

He swallowed before answering, "You know."

Her belly flip-flopped. The Gods forgive her, she did.

Ava did her best to mask her reaction, even as sweat beaded on her skin and her pulse went wild. Moving away from the cabinet, she crossed to where he was standing by the reading desk, halting when they were around three feet apart. "We shouldn't talk about this," she said firmly.

Captain Jax held her gaze. "Why not?"

"I told you why … earlier."

"Is there a reason why you're up reading when you should be sleeping?" he asked. "Or am I not the only one with insomnia?"

Ava didn't want to discuss that either. Murmuring a curse under her breath, she clenched her hands by her sides. "We have to stop this conversation, Jax," she whispered. "We're both standing on the edge of a cliff right now … one misstep and we'll go over."

16. NO ONE CAN HEAR US

AS SOON AS Ava spoke those words, as soon as she called him by his first name, she wished she could call them back.

She'd just admitted that she wanted him, and he was looking at her now like he wanted to devour her.

Silence swelled between them, the tension drawing tighter still.

Eventually, Captain Jax shattered it. "I didn't want this either," he admitted, closing the remaining gap between them. "My life was much easier before I met you."

"As was mine before you crashed into it," she answered, cursing the way her voice hitched.

They were standing so close now she could feel the heat of his body enveloping her. His smell, woodsy yet at the same time dark and spicy, made her breathing grow shallower still. Her chest rose and fell sharply.

"I used to have my shit together," he ground out, his gaze never leaving hers. "But these days, I can't concentrate on anything but you." His face twisted as if he were in physical pain. "What have you done to me, woman?"

"Nothing," Ava whispered back, even as an ache of longing rose under her breastbone. "I didn't want you here, remember?"

His nostrils flared. "And now?"

"I wish you'd never set foot on this planet." The words rushed out of her. "You're always in my face, always challenging me, pushing me. Gods, I wish I'd never met you."

That last line came out in a cry, her voice cracking. Her lips parted once more as she readied herself to rail at him again. However, Ava never managed to—for he reached out, his fingers gripping her shoulders, and hauled her against him.

A beat later, his hard mouth was on hers.

And just like that, the tension that had been building between them for weeks now exploded.

All rational thought fled Ava's mind. The only thing she could focus on was him—on his big muscular body against her own, on the way his mouth savaged hers. He tasted like life, like sin, and he set her on fire. She kissed him back wildly, their teeth clashing and tongues tangling.

Need crashed into Ava with dizzying force. Her hands slid up his chest, splaying across the thick material of his body suit. Her fingernails dug in. She wanted to rip it off him, wanted to taste the hot skin underneath.

As if sensing her desperation, Jax drew back, his grip on her shoulders tightening as he stared down at her face. He was breathing hard, and his expression was fierce. "I shouldn't have done that," he rasped. One hand left her shoulder then, cupping her chin with surprising gentleness. "This is wrong. I know it … but I can't stop myself. You need to tell me to go, Ava, or I'm going to pick you up, carry you into your solar, and fuck you senseless."

Her breathing hitched, dizziness sweeping over her once more.

She *should* tell him to leave, should push him away from her. He was giving her the opportunity to stop things from going further, yet the voice of reason that was screaming somewhere in the back of her mind was drowned out by a wild hunger.

The Gods forgive her, she *wanted* him to fuck her senseless.

She craved it.

"Don't go," she gasped. "Please."

And that was all she had to say before he pulled her against him again, his mouth slanting over hers. His tongue then parted her lips, gliding against hers. Ava groaned. Yes, she couldn't give this up. She had to experience everything Jax had to give. Just once.

His arms went around her then, sliding down the curve of her back to the swell of her backside. True to his word, he picked her up, letting her wrap her legs around his hips. The position was shockingly intimate, and despite the layers of clothing that separated them, the rock-hard length of his erection pressed against her core.

Ava whimpered.

"Keep making sounds like that, Ava, and we aren't going to make it to the solar," he growled.

With that, Jax headed down the aisle, between the reading desks and illuminated cabinets of ancient books, toward the door at the far end of the library. Each stride brought their bodies hard up against each other.

The friction was delicious, and Ava bit down on her lower lip to stop herself from whimpering again. She wanted him to take her inside the solar, in private. There weren't any security-cams in the library and most of those residing inside the temple were asleep right now. Nonetheless, someone could walk in on them.

The door to the solar whispered open to admit them before Jax slammed the heel of his hand against the panel inside, locking it.

Their mouths found each other once more, and they kissed hungrily while Jax walked across the wide floor toward the cushion-covered dais, heeling his boots off as he went. They thudded on the carpeted floor, yet he kicked them aside, his mouth never leaving Ava's. He sat her on the edge of the dais, and then he was stripping off her clothing. Her tunic, bra, and leggings all hit the floor with remarkable speed, leaving her naked in front of him, save for the gleaming obsidian pendant between her breasts.

The lights were soft inside the solar, just a couple of wall globes illuminated the cavernous space. However, there was no hiding from him.

Jax's ebony eyes gleamed as his gaze dragged down the length of her, taking in the heavy swell of her breasts and the curves of her hips, belly, and thighs.

Ava's breathing was coming in short, needy pants now. She'd never felt beautiful before, yet she did under his hot stare. He looked at her as if she were the Goddess Miradia herself.

Murmuring a curse, he sank to his knees on the floor before the dais. He then cupped her breasts, pushing them up so that they thrust in his face, before leaning in.

Ava groaned as his tongue stroked each nipple and his teeth grazed them. And when he began to suck hard, her strangled cry echoed across the solar. She caught herself then, slamming a hand over her mouth.

Jax glanced up, favoring her with a heated look. "Make all the noise you want in here," he murmured. "No one can hear us."

He was right, of course. With the roar of the wind outdoors, any sounds they made would be drowned out. They were far from the accommodation areas anyway.

Meeting his eye, she nodded.

Jax ducked his head once more. And this time, when his hungry mouth suckled her, Ava didn't stop herself from groaning, from crying out. She even encouraged him, in guttural whispers, her hands cradling the back of his head, her fingers sliding through his short dark hair. Her words encouraged him, excited him, and he suckled her harder still, until Ava was arching against him.

When he drew back, they were both breathing hard.

Gently, Jax pushed her down onto the cushions, his mouth traveling down the deep valley between her breasts to her navel. And then, as her breathing grew ragged and her pulse thundered in her ears, he pushed her trembling thighs apart and nestled his face between them.

The flick of his tongue brought her up off the cushions with a cry, yet he didn't let up. Instead, he tasted her there, sucking and licking until Ava completely forgot herself.

Gasping his name, she ground herself against his face, writhing as pleasure wound tighter in her lower belly, building steadily.

One of his hands glided along her inner thigh. He then slid a thick finger inside her, sinking deep. Moments later, a second finger joined the first, and he slowly thrust them in and out of her, curling his fingers upward as he did so.

Ava's stomach muscles clenched, and she choked out a curse.

Gasping, she curled upward, her hands clutching at him. She wasn't sure what she wanted—whether she wanted him to stop or keep going—only that the sensations he provoked in her were so powerful they scared her. "Jax!"

He glanced up, his mouth curving. "It's okay," he murmured. "I've got you, Ava … just relax into it … ride it."

Their gazes fused for a moment, and then she nodded. She trusted him, although letting go wasn't something she'd ever found easy.

Sinking back onto the cushions, she let her eyes flutter closed as he resumed his delicious torture. She was slowly inching toward the edge. It was incredible. She couldn't believe she'd gone her entire life without experiencing pleasure like this.

Her whole body had turned liquid as he steadily brought her higher and higher. Aching pleasure exploded then, twisting and pulsing through the cradle of her hips. Ava shuddered and bucked against him, while he continued to flick his tongue against her, riding the waves of pleasure until she collapsed, shaking, against the cushions.

Jax rose up between her thighs, climbing to his feet.

Then, his gaze never leaving her face, he undid his weapons holsters and lowered them to the floor. After that, he unfastened his body suit, peeling it off to reveal the hard-muscled body underneath.

Ava watched, transfixed. Pale skin gleamed in the soft light, and her gaze alighted upon a tattoo: a great serpent that wound its way up his left arm, across his chest, ending just above his groin.

And when he pushed down his body suit further, revealing all of him, his cock sprang up, released from its prison.

Ava's breathing caught. He was magnificent. She'd already realized he was big, but the sight of his shaft, thick, tapering, and curved, thrusting up from his groin like a weapon, shocked her. And then, when he saw her staring, and fisted it, sliding his hand up and down the shaft, moisture beaded on the swollen tip.

Swallowing, Ava tore her attention from his groin and met his eye.

Jax's gaze was hooded, his lips parted, as he watched her. "Is this your first time?" he asked.

Ava nodded, nervousness and excitement both thrumming through her.

She might have been a virgin, but she wasn't an innocent. She knew what would happen next and ached for it. She ached for *him*.

Wordlessly, she shifted back on the cushions, moving to the center of the dais. She then spread her legs for him once more, watching as his chest rose and fell sharply now, his gaze fixed between her thighs.

"Jax," she whispered. "Please."

An instant later, he was there, pushing her thighs wide, and sliding the slick head of his cock into her.

Ava gasped, wriggling against him as he worked his way inside. She was ready for him, but he was big.

She'd expected this to hurt, yet it didn't. Nonetheless, he was a tight fit, and it took a while—as he rolled his hips and steadily bore down on her—for him to slide in to the hilt. And when he did, Ava's legs were stretched so wide her hip muscles risked cramping. He filled her completely; there didn't feel as if there was a millimeter to spare.

Her breathing grew shallow, worry rising. Could she handle this?

"Just relax, Ava … I won't hurt you," Jax murmured. Reaching between them, he gently stroked her where their bodies met. Pleasure throbbed through her loins, and she lifted her hips slightly, grinding against him. The act made the pleasure intensify. Ava cried out, trembling as he slowly withdrew, almost to the tip, before bearing down on her once more.

And then, before Ava knew it, he was fucking her, deep and slow, while something quickened within her. It was a melting, throbbing sensation that grew each time he thrust home.

Ava was aware that she was now crying out, her gasps and groans echoing through the solar and blending with the whine of the wind and the rattling of the shutters. The sounds she was making were raw and feral, yet she couldn't stop herself.

Jax growled a string of the dirtiest words she'd ever heard then. Her reaction stripped him of restraint, and he started to drive into her, faster and harder.

It was too much, and Ava shattered, a scream tearing from her throat.

17. CRAVING

FOR A LONG while after her climax, Ava felt as if she were floating.

Lying splayed across Jax's sweat-slicked chest and torso, her legs tangled with his, she was limp, boneless. Her solar seemed to be rotating slowly around her, and her pulse thudded in her ears. She couldn't have gotten up, even if the temple were burning down around her.

She didn't speak, didn't move—and, likewise, Jax remained still and silent.

After they'd both come, he'd sprawled out on the cushions atop the dais before dragging her on top of him. And they'd lain like that ever since.

Eventually though, as the minutes ticked by, the torpor that wrapped them in its embrace lifted.

Reality crept back in like a cold mist tickling at their naked limbs.

Ava stirred first, lifting her cheek from his chest, and propping herself up on an elbow. Jax stared up at her. His expression was veiled, yet his black eyes burned into her.

Swallowing, Ava slid her hand over his chest, her fingertips tracing the serpent tattoo that had been inked there. "When did you get this?"

His mouth quirked. "When I was thirteen ... it's a tradition upon Morvin, for young males to have The Serpent, Volidas, tattooed on them. The fire snake protects, guides, and" —his smile inched a little wider— "ensures virility."

"It's quite a tattoo," she admitted, inspecting the detail of the scales and spikes that bristled along the serpent's back. "It must have taken a while to do?"

"A few sessions."

Ava fell silent. Although his tattoo had intrigued her, this wasn't the time to discuss it. Her chest constricted then. Gods, why was nothing ever easy? Ava had told herself for years that she wasn't missing out, that sex was messy and awkward, but what she'd just experienced with Jax was life-changing. How was she supposed to go on as normal now? How could she accept the austerity of her life, knowing what could have been?

She swallowed hard. It was foolish to ask herself such questions. She had to go on—she had no choice, did she?

"It's okay, Ava ... I know this can't happen again," Jax said softly, filling the void between them.

Ava released the breath she hadn't even realized she'd been holding. She then nodded. "I fought it so hard," she whispered, "but I should have realized it was impossible."

He reached up a hand, his large palm cupping her cheek. "It's not your fault."

His words made the ache in her chest deepen. "Now you understand why I need to keep away from you?" she asked hoarsely.

He nodded. "From now on, I'll start eating at the table with my warriors." He paused then, his features tightening. "I don't want to put your position here at risk."

Ava cleared her throat. "Or yours?"

He nodded, his features tightening. Clearly, he'd considered that too.

"We need to remember why you're here," Ava said, forcing herself on. "To protect me ... and this temple ... against *The Creed*."

"I've never forgotten," he murmured. "But you're right ... whatever this is between us ... it's a distraction. It could get you killed."

They both fell silent once more as the time slowly inched by.

A chill crawled over Ava's skin then. It wasn't her own life she worried about the most—but what this forbidden encounter could mean for the order.

They didn't need any more instability right now. It hit her then that *she* was a threat to the Temple of the

Gods—her behavior could play right into the hands of the extremists.

"What's the time?" she asked huskily.

Jax glanced down at the wrist-comm still strapped to his right wrist. "We've got an hour before breakfast," he replied. "We should both get back to our quarters."

Ava nodded, placing her hand over where his left hand still cupped her cheek. Gently, she pulled back and turned his hand over, brushing her lips across his scarred knuckles. Suddenly, it hurt to breathe. She knew this was wrong, yet she still didn't want to let go. "I won't forget this, Jax," she whispered. "Ever."

His breathing quickened just a fraction. "Neither will I," he replied.

"Mistress Ava." DD-J3 greeted her the moment she strode into her bedchamber. "I was concerned as to your whereabouts."

Forcing a smile, Ava headed toward the bathroom. "No need, Dee Dee … I was meditating in my solar and fell asleep."

"Did Captain Jax not locate you?"

"He did … but I sent him away."

Lights flashed on the droid's domed head as it processed her response. "Why did you not respond to your wrist-comm, Mistress Ava?"

Ava sighed, halting so that she could focus on her droid. Dee Dee could be annoyingly persistent, and this morning was one of those times. "You know I switch it off when I'm meditating."

"So, all is well, My Lady?"

Ava nodded. "All is well."

Her stomach twisted. No, it wasn't. She'd broken her vows. She'd succumbed to lust and given herself to the Captain of the Guardians of the Flame, had let him fuck her upon her meditation dais without an instant of shame. She'd welcomed his touch, had craved it. And, curse her, she still did.

Her sisters and the Wise Ones might not know what she'd done last night, but the Gods would. Eventually, they'd punish her for it.

Nausea washed over Ava. She and Jax hadn't used any protection either. As soon as she'd had a quick shower, she'd need to head to the infirmary. At this hour, there were only droids on duty there. She'd be able to help herself to medication that would prevent pregnancy without Sister Thelia noticing.

Turning from Dee Dee, she entered the bathroom without another word. She then switched the shower on and stepped under scalding needles of water, trying to wash her shame away. But she couldn't. And there was part of her that didn't want to.

If she was honest with herself, she wanted to keep Jax's scent on her skin and hold the memories of their encounter forever. She didn't want to forget the details, of how he'd tasted, how he'd felt, buried inside her, or of the deep, masculine sound of his groans of pleasure.

Yet, she knew she would, eventually.

Misery twisted her up inside as she deftly washed. Then, stepping out of the shower, glowing pink, she pulled on clean clothing and hurried from her quarters.

Dee Dee let her go without comment, which was a relief. Lying to the droid, which had faithfully served her for so many years, just made her feel worse.

Jax watched one of his warriors spar with Lady Ava.

There had been recent reports of *The Creed* mobilizing in a nearby system. As such, Jax had lengthened the combat training sessions for all the

Sisters of Awe. He'd also increased the patrols on-planet and throughout the system.

Something was coming, and they all had to be ready for it.

The two women wielded laser-blades. Their weapons, set to stun, glowed blue in the eternal twilight. This afternoon, he'd pitted her against Thresha, one of his best. Ava's skill with a laser-blade had improved significantly over the past weeks. However, she'd asked for a challenge, and so he'd given her one.

Thresha, a tall, lithe human female with long, braided black hair and golden eyes, moved with lethal fluidity.

Jax had thought Ava wouldn't last five minutes against her. Yet, here they were, ten minutes into their bout, and the High Priestess was still holding her own.

They were outdoors, on the wide viewing terrace they now used as their training space. It was unusually still this afternoon, with only a slight breeze stirring the cool air.

As such, both women were sweating.

Ava's bare arms gleamed as she swung her blade around to deflect a hard strike from her opponent.

A smile tugged at Jax's mouth. *I taught her that move.*

He had—although the memory of the hours they'd spent alone together practicing held a sting these days.

Jax's mood darkened.

A week had passed since that forbidden night. A week to consider his behavior and to berate himself for it.

He was a fucking idiot. He should have known better, but somehow, that night he'd lost control. It had been a mistake, for instead of easing his ache for Ava, it had merely stoked it. And now that he'd had a taste of her, he needed more.

But it was a craving that could go nowhere. One with no future.

Jax knew that, yet it didn't stop his gaze from tracking Ava as she fought. Gods, she looked good today, dressed in a sleeveless black bodysuit, her pale skin flushed and gleaming.

The sight reminded him of what she'd looked like naked, spread out underneath him. He'd never seen anything so beautiful as watching while Ava gave up her hard-won control.

Fuck.

His groin had swollen and was now pressing painfully against his armor.

He clenched his jaw. This wasn't the time or place for a hard-on. He was standing on the edge of the terrace, flanked by a few of his guards. A crowd had gathered to watch Ava and Thresha spar, even a handful of priestesses had left their duties to observe the spectacle.

He couldn't let himself fantasize about Ava like this, or he'd slowly go crazy. Ever since their encounter, they'd done as they'd agreed and kept apart. If his warriors or her sisters noticed that the High Priestess and Captain Jax didn't take meals or train together anymore, and no longer met to update each other, no one said anything.

The hum and crack of the laser-blades colliding filled the air as each woman fought for dominance.

Thresha eventually bested Ava, getting under her guard and knocking her onto her back with a strike to the abdomen.

Ava skidded backward across the smooth surface of the terrace, her laser-blade flying from her hand. It bounced across stone, and Jax stepped forward, scooping up the weapon. He then crossed the terrace to Ava, and without thinking, held out a hand to her.

"My Lady ... are you hurt?"

Breathing hard, Ava shook her head. She stared up at him, those pewter eyes wide.

Jax could almost hear her silent rebuke: *what are you doing?* They weren't supposed to have any contact, and yet here he was offering her his hand.

And she couldn't refuse it without drawing attention to them both.

"I'm fine," she gasped. "Just a bruised pride, that's all."

"No need to feel bad, My Lady," Thresha announced, striding up to them. The warrior had a wide grin upon her face. "That was the best fight I've had in a long while."

Ava smiled back, even as she took Jax's hand and allowed him to draw her to her feet. "Right then … do you want to go another round?"

18. AN HONOR

STANDING AT THE edge of the landing platform, Ava adjusted her cloak before brushing the dust off her skirts.

"Stop fidgeting, Ava," Skylar murmured to her, careful to keep her voice low so no one else could hear them. "You look fine."

Huffing a sigh, Ava glanced her Second's way. As usual, Skylar appeared regal and composed.

She'll make a good High Priestess one day.

The thought caught Ava unawares. It was a foolish one, for they were of a similar age, and there wasn't any reason why Ava wouldn't lead the order for many more years. When it was time to hand over the mantle to another, the Wise Ones would likely choose a much younger successor.

"I'm nervous," she admitted, with a grimace. "It's not every day we get a visit from clan leaders."

"It's certainly an honor."

"It is … although an unexpected one." No clan leader had visited the temple in all her years on Pillarus One. As such, she'd been surprised by their announcement just two days earlier.

"Look … here they come," Skylar said, pointing upward.

Squinting up at the sky, Ava caught sight of three shuttles approaching. All three descended at the same level, yet as they drew closer, she noted that the one on the far left was a golden Mir-Brennan craft, the next was Mir-Ferrin bronze, and the last one was a silver Mir-Lelith shuttle. It surprised her to see the leaders arriving separately, although, on second thought, it was likely safer.

It was also a reminder that until recently, the three clans had been in conflict.

The shuttles landed, blowing stinging particles of dust into the faces of the priestesses and warriors who encircled the wide landing platform. As the craft shut down their engines, Ava glanced away, her gaze seeking out Jax.

She should be ignoring him right now, as she had done for the last couple of weeks successfully, but she wanted to know his reaction.

The clan leaders had planned this visit at the last minute, possibly to avoid *The Creed of Truth* hearing about it. As such, Jax had been busy ever since getting things ready for their arrival.

He was standing around ten meters away, flanked by two of his warriors. Jax was clad in full armor and regalia, as he had been on the day they'd met. His fine crimson cloak billowed as the shuttles' engines died to a whine and then fell silent.

An ache rose under Ava's breastbone. The only part of his face she could see was his strong jaw and serious mouth. However, it made her long to push her way through the line of priestesses and warriors separating them and wrap her arms around him.

The impulse was so strong that she found herself clenching her fists at her sides.

Gods, she missed him. She kept busy, but it wasn't enough. There were still many quiet moments in the day when longing would creep in, like a thief, and torment her.

She missed the rumble of his voice. The way he questioned her, challenged her. His protectiveness that she found both irritating and reassuring. And she missed being physically close to him. Not just the sex—for that had been a stolen, forbidden time—but sitting next to him at mealtimes and training.

She missed it all so badly that it hurt to breathe.

She was sure Jax wouldn't notice her look his way, as his attention was riveted elsewhere, sure it was safe to sneak a glance at him—but his head turned to her.

His visor was down, but despite that, she felt his gaze burn into her, felt the force of his stare.

Ava's mouth went dry, and it was only the hiss of hydraulics, as the shuttle hatches lowered, that made her jerk her attention away.

A woman appeared from the Mir-Brennan shuttle. Small with long brown hair, she wore long golden robes and held herself regally. An instant later, a tall man clad in a bronze tunic and leggings strode down the ramp from the Mir-Ferrin craft. The last of the clan-leaders to emerge was a rawboned middle-aged man, clad in flowing silver.

Jenna Mir-Brennan, Elijah Mir-Ferrin, and Aran Mir-Lelith had arrived.

"Your security measures are impressive, Captain." Lady Jenna turned from where she'd been viewing the row of proximity beacons planted around the entrance to the temple, to face Jax, favoring him with a nod.

"Thank you, My Lady," he replied.

Jax didn't add that he'd have preferred more time to prepare for their visit. He didn't like surprises. It felt as if the clan leaders were trying to catch him out.

"Your team is doing a good job," Lord Elijah spoke up then. "And with a security net around the planet, you've got the first line of defense sorted."

"*The Creed* knows how to deal with security nets," Lord Aran pointed out. The Mir-Lelith clan-lord stood at the rear of the small group Jax had led through the temple and around its base. "You better not be relying on that to stop them."

"We aren't, My Lord," Jax assured him, even as irritation rose. "Thanks to your generosity, My Lord, all our cruisers are fitted with the latest weaponry." He paused then, his gaze flicking to where Ava stood next to him. During the tour, she'd remained silent, letting him take the lead. "The Sisters of Awe are taking the threat seriously. They are now all combat-trained and armed."

He didn't add that he'd had to bully them all into training.

Three pairs of gazes shifted to Lady Ava, marking the laser-blade that hung from her belt.

Jenna Mir-Brennan then frowned. "Is arming the Sisters of Awe necessary?"

"I wasn't overjoyed about the idea either," Ava admitted with a half-smile. "But Captain Jax quickly convinced me of its importance." She then patted the laser-blade grip. "I must admit I feel safer here knowing I can use this."

"Lady Ava has some skill," Jax added, unable to help himself. Ava was unlikely to brag about her ability, so he'd do it for her.

All three of the clan leaders nodded at his statement. Nonetheless, Lady Jenna still didn't appear convinced. Like many, she was likely superstitious about arming the Sisters of Awe.

Eventually, Ava cleared her throat. "With your permission, I shall lead you back inside now. We have time for a meeting before the evening meal."

"Of course," Lord Elijah replied with an easy smile.

"Very well," Lord Aran added, although his expression was slightly irritated. "I can't stay long though. As soon as we've had our meeting, I'll be leaving."

The Mir-Ferrin clan-lord cast him a sharp look. "I thought we'd all agreed to stay the night?"

The Mir-Lelith clan-lord shrugged. "I had … but on the way here, I received reports of *The Creed* sacking temples to Aura and Jidea in the system next to Caldoros. I can't afford to stay away too long."

"There have been problems in our territories as well, Aran," The Mir-Brennan clan-lady replied crisply. "That's why we agreed to meet."

Jax's gaze narrowed as he watched the dynamic between the three clan leaders. It was becoming clear that Lady Jenna and Lord Elijah had pressured the Mir-Lelith clan-lord into making this trip. Ever since disembarking from his gleaming silver shuttle, Lord Aran had been grumpy and obstructive.

"And I have." Lord Aran's jaw tightened as he met Jenna Mir-Brennan's eye. "We should be able to discuss all that's necessary this afternoon, anyway." He shifted his attention to the High Priestess then, dismissing the clan-lady. "Lead the way, Lady Ava."

19. TRULY ALONE

SEATED AT A large circular table in her solar, Ava observed the clan leaders with interest.

None of them were what she'd expected.

Lady Jenna was warm yet with a no-nonsense manner. Ava had heard she'd once been a diplomat before her brother's untimely death saw her elevated to the position of clan-lady. She had a soft appearance, yet there was no missing the steely glint in her brown eyes when she addressed the other two clan leaders.

Of course, as a Mir-Brennan herself, Ava was always going to be more kindly disposed toward Lady Jenna. Nonetheless, she'd been surprised by Elijah Mir-Ferrin. Handsome and suave, he came from a line of ruthless leaders, clan-lords driven by a lust for power. But Lord Elijah was different, somehow. There was a balance to him that she'd witnessed in his comments during Jax's tour of the temple's defenses.

The one she was the least sure about was Lord Aran. He was irritable, impatient, and openly distrustful of Lady Jenna and Lord Elijah. However, to their credit, they both appeared patient with him, as if they were used to his ways.

Aran Mir-Lelith drummed his fingertips on the polished tabletop in front of him now. They'd just finished going over all the recent intel their agents had picked up on *The Creed of Truth*. However, Mir-Lelith was plainly impatient to be on his way.

"*The Creed* must never set foot on this planet," he announced. "If those terrorists ever managed to damage the temple, it would cause chaos throughout the sector."

"That's why we created the Guardians of the Flame, Aran," Lady Jenna reminded him gently. "We're all aware of the danger … and why I arranged this visit."

Ava inclined her head. So, the Mir-Brennan clan-lady was behind this, was she?

"May I speak freely?" Jax spoke up then, the deep timbre of his voice carrying across the solar.

All gazes swiveled to him before Elijah Mir-Ferrin nodded. "Go on, Captain."

Jax nodded to him. "We can put up all the walls we want, but it won't stop *The Creed* from gaining strength, from recruiting others into their ranks. Our position is too defensive. If we sit here waiting long enough, they'll find a way to knock our walls down. We need more resources so that we can actively engage them."

Lord Aran gave a soft snort. "I'm sure you would, Captain. However, we've already supplied you with more than enough ships, weaponry, and soldiers. What do you want, your own personal army?"

Jax's jaw tightened. "No, My Lord."

"Well, just do the job we hired you for ... and leave the strategizing to those in charge."

A heavy silence fell in the solar.

Ava's gaze narrowed. It was a rude response; Lord Aran's tone implied that the Captain of the Guardians of the Flame was greedy and overly ambitious.

Jax didn't answer, and Ava admired him for his self-control. In his place, she wasn't sure she'd have been able to hold her tongue. Clan-lord or not, Aran Mir-Lelith seemed to have forgotten his manners.

Meanwhile, the other two clan leaders stiffened in their seats. "I wouldn't have put it so bluntly ... but Lord Aran has a point," Elijah Mir-Ferrin said finally, his handsome face veiling. "The situation near Caldoros has shown that any extra resources need to be put into protecting our key planets and space stations."

Across from him, Jenna Mir-Brennan gave a slow nod. "I agree, Elijah." Her gaze turned steely as it rested upon Jax. "There might come a time when we'll need to launch an offensive against *The Creed* ... but for now they're scattered across the sector and almost impossible to track. A defensive position is the wisest one at present."

"Fucking idiots."

Ava cut Jax a sharp look.

They were standing on the landing platform outside the temple, watching as the last of the three shuttles disappeared, lights winking, into space. In the end, all three clan leaders had left after supper. Behind the High Priestess and captain stood ranks of helmed warriors. Since the wind roared around them now, it was unlikely any of them had heard Jax.

But Ava had.

"Their decision is final, Jax," she reminded him gently. "There's no point in fighting it."

He shoved up his visor and turned to her. "So, you agree with the clan leaders?"

Ava gave a soft snort. "No. For the record, I think you put forward a valid argument. They just didn't to hear it."

Jax's black gaze bored into hers, and as their stare drew out, Ava's heart started to pound.

Gods, it was still there, as strong as before, this violent pull between them.

They couldn't remain out here though. Now that the shuttles had departed, nothing was keeping them out on this platform.

Today had brought them together briefly, but it was time to go indoors.

Back to their separate routines.

Inside her solar, Ava shed her cloak and climbed up onto the dais. Usually, she changed into leggings before meditating, as they were more comfortable, but this evening, she didn't bother.

Today had unsettled Ava. The clan leaders' visit and the discussions that followed had highlighted the growing threat *The Creed* presented. For years, she'd lived as if the rest of the sector, indeed the galaxy, didn't exist. But now there was no ignoring the problems that went on elsewhere—problems that would come here if not checked.

However, it wasn't just the discussions with the clan leaders that had put her on edge—spending time with Jax today had knocked her off balance as well. She needed to find her equilibrium once more.

Withdrawing the Amulet of the Gods from under her clothing, Ava held it up to the bloody light filtering through the wide windows. She slowed down her breathing, centering herself and letting her mind quiet, before slowly slipping into a reflective state.

She'd spent a lot of time meditating, of late.

It soothed her worries, lifted her up and carried her to a place where only light and serenity existed. Where the Gods could speak to her. Sometimes, she could hear the rumble and whisper of their voices, but not this evening.

During this session, there was only silence. And when Ava finally emerged a while later, unease tickled at the back of her mind. She hoped she wasn't losing her fragile connection with the Gods.

If that happened, the Wise Ones would choose another to lead the order.

Trying not to worry, Ava left her solar and made her way up to her quarters.

Dee Dee was there, folding clean clothes by the bed. "Good evening, Mistress," it chirped.

"Evening, Dee Dee." The flatness of her voice surprised her. She wasn't herself tonight.

Her droid clearly thought so too, for it turned to her, lights blinking on its domed head. "Is something wrong, Mistress?"

"I'm not sure," she replied with a sigh. "Could you run me a bath and add perfumed oil to it?"

"Of course." Dee Dee trundled off into the bathroom to do her bidding, and moments later, she heard the rush of water. Meanwhile, Ava sank down onto the bed, staring sightlessly out the window.

The wind had gotten up further since the clan leaders had left. Tiny whirlwinds scattered crazily across the valley in front of the temple, dancing on the gleaming surface of the landing platform. Captain Jax's shuttle sat there now, crouched like a grey insect as the wind buffeted it.

Heaviness pressed down on her. How tired she got of the eternal dusk and the howling wind here. She longed to see the sunset or to feel the hot midday sun on her face like other planets. The stasis was a constant reminder that this planet was dying. It made her feel trapped, suffocated.

Ava's breathing grew shallow. The sensation reminded her of how she'd often felt before Jax Mir-Lelith's arrival. Somehow, his presence chased away her loneliness and the sense of isolation, her lingering fear that this position might turn her mad, as it had done Keisha.

But this evening, there was no denying that she was truly alone.

"Commander, we've picked up something on the security net monitor."

"What is it, Ensign?"

Commander Asher of *The Star-Hawk* moved over to the console, peering down at where the outline of the planet they guarded glowed, surrounded by an array of blinking lights.

"It looks like a meteor, Sir."

Asher's gaze narrowed as he watched the speck arrow through space. In seconds, it would hit the planet's atmosphere. "Where did that come from?" he demanded, his voice sharpening.

"Out of nowhere, Commander. It just appeared onscreen."

Asher scowled. His pulse then quickened. "What's its trajectory?"

"It'll hit twenty klicks south of the temple, Sir."

"That's too close." He swiveled on his heel, his gaze spearing the officer sitting behind them. "Lieutenant Trega," he barked. "Launch a pyro-torpedo and deal with it."

The Crall nodded, his bulbous eyes blinking. "Aye, Commander." His long fingers then danced across the screen in front of him.

"It's just hit the planet's atmosphere, Sir," the ensign said, her voice tightening. "Wait … it's caught fire."

Asher leaned forward once more, his gaze alighting on the blur onscreen. All his senses were sharp now, on high alert. However, he reminded himself it wasn't uncommon for a meteorite to burn up upon entering a planet's atmosphere. Maybe there wasn't any cause for concern, after all. "Status report?"

The ensign's fingers tapped the screen before she let out the breath she'd been holding. "It's gone, Sir. All that will hit the planet will be ash and debris."

The tension in the commander's shoulders eased, and his pulse slowed. He hadn't liked the look of that meteorite, or the way it had come out of nowhere. His crew had charted all nearby meteorites and asteroid fields. How had they missed that one?

"Good," he murmured, unease still prickling his skin. He then glanced over his shoulder at Lieutenant Trega. "Terminate the missile launch, Lieutenant."

The Crall nodded. "Aye, Sir."

Tense moments passed, and then Asher turned back to the ensign. "Log it, nonetheless, and I'll let Captain Jax know. It always pays to be careful."

The gleaming black pod fell from the sky and crashed into a narrow ravine, tunneling through dry, hard earth before coming to a halt nearly two klicks from where it had hit.

Smoke and steam rose from its smooth cylindrical sides.

A minute passed before the pod split apart like an egg, and a spindly metal figure unfolded itself from it.

The droid rose to its feet, its body changing from black to a tawny brown to match its surroundings. Twin golden eyes swept the vicinity, and then it climbed from the wreckage of the pod.

Pausing once more, the droid scanned for threats, its metal body crouching slightly, readying itself to draw a weapon. However, it found no danger in the vicinity. The entry had been successful. A security net ringed this planet, so someone would have seen it enter the planet's atmosphere, but the cloaking device should have done its job, making the pod look like a stray meteorite.

The droid's scans revealed that it was twenty-one klicks from the Temple of the Gods. Its planned trajectory had been perfect.

It began to walk north, covering the rocky ground in long strides, while it continued to scan its environs.

Tall and thin, the color of its metal body constantly changing to blend into the nearby rocks, the droid knew it was hard to spot. However, it would have numerous threats to deal with on its way to the temple.

The droid's pace quickened, its rubber-soled feet crunching on pebbles.

Patrols or proximity beacons wouldn't stop it from reaching its destination and achieving its purpose.

Nothing would.

20. UNCHAINED

JAX HAD JUST terminated a call with Commander Asher, and was about to contact the guards currently on patrol south of the temple, when the comm to his chamber buzzed.

He stiffened, while on the wall, his utility-droid came to life with a whir and a fluttering of lights. "Shall I answer that, Sir?" it chirped.

"It's all right DT-45, I'll do it." Rising from where he'd been sitting on the edge of the bed, Jax pulled on a loose pair of pants and padded over to the door. He then pressed the comm. "Who is it?"

"Captain?" A woman's voice, husky and low, filtered into his chamber. "Can I come in?"

Ava.

Without hesitating, Jax punched the panel under the comm, and the door whispered open.

Indeed, the High Priestess stood there. Barefoot and dressed in a long, sleeveless tunic, Ava's face was composed. However, her grey eyes were luminous in the overhead light.

Jax frowned, stepping forward and peering into the corridor behind her. It was empty. "My Lady?"

"It's all right … no one knows I'm here," she replied softly. "I waited until the patrol passed before slipping out of my chamber."

Jax's brow furrowed. It wasn't a long journey between their quarters—for he'd insisted from the beginning that he had to be lodged close to the High Priestess. All the same, she'd taken a risk in visiting him like this. What if one of the security-cams picked her up?

He'd need to check them tomorrow and delete anything incriminating.

In the meantime, it was clear Ava wasn't leaving. Jax drew back, his gaze searching her face once more before he motioned for her to enter his chamber.

She did, and when the door closed, Jax turned to her. "What's wrong?"

She met his eye, and the impact of it made his gut clench. She was testing his willpower severely. Before Commander Asher's call, he'd been lying awake, staring up into the darkness, trying not to think about her.

They'd had a lot of contact today—too much contact.

And now here Ava was, standing just a couple of feet from him. All he had to do was reach out and haul her into his arms.

However, he didn't.

"I woke you up, sorry," she murmured. A faint blush rose to her cheeks. Since he'd opened the door, she'd kept her attention on his face, almost as if she was deliberately avoiding looking at the rest of him. Of course, he *was* half-naked.

"You didn't," he grunted. "That reminds me ... I was about to make a call. Can you wait a moment?"

Ava nodded, swallowing. She looked nervous, as if she wished she hadn't made this visit. Soon, he'd get to the bottom of it. However, first, he had to ensure the perimeter was secure.

He stabbed at his wrist-comm. "Lieutenant Thresher."

"Yes, Sir." The woman's voice answered seconds later.

"The security net has picked up a meteorite. It entered the atmosphere around twenty klicks south of the temple, although it appeared to disintegrate on entry. All the same, I want you to check it out."

"Yes, Sir."

"I'll send you through the exact coordinates now."

Jax cut the call, and with a couple of taps of his fingertip, forwarded the coordinates Lieutenant Asher had sent.

He then glanced up to find Ava watching him, a groove etched between her brows. "Is something wrong?"

He shook his head. "Probably not ... although since the meteorite seemed to come from nowhere, I want to be sure it's not anything sinister." He moved forward then, closing the gap between them. "Now ... you have my full attention, Ava."

Gods, it felt as if a rock sat on her chest.

What was she doing standing in Captain Jax's bedchamber? The man had answered the door barely clothed, and despite that she'd kept her gaze on his face, one glance at his heavily muscled chest and torso, and the tattoo that wrapped itself sinuously around him, and her pulse had gone wild.

You're losing your mind.

Maybe she was, but she couldn't stand it any longer.

She'd tried not to think about him. She'd had a long bath, and then she'd gone to bed and attempted to get some sleep. But that was a joke. She couldn't sleep. Now that her mind had fixed on Jax, it wouldn't let go.

Eventually, she hadn't been able to stand it any longer.

She'd gotten up, thrown on a tunic, and headed for the door.

Of course, Dee Dee had wanted to know where she was going. She'd lied, telling the utility-droid that since she was having trouble sleeping, she was going to her solar to meditate.

Her droid had accepted her explanation without questioning her further, and guilt had speared Ava. What was she doing, sneaking around and lying to her faithful Dee Dee?

But here she was, and she had a couple of choices right now.

She could make a lame excuse and leave, or she could tell Jax the truth.

"I can't go on like this," she whispered deciding that she wouldn't be a coward. She'd made it this far; she might as well say the words that burned within her. "I miss you."

His black eyes snapped wide at this admission, and his breathing grew shallow. "Ava," he whispered. "This is a bad idea."

Heat flushed through her. Gods, she was an idiot. Now he'd be worrying how to deal with this needy woman, who'd just turned up at his door in the middle of the night. "You're right," she said, cursing the way her voice caught. "I should go."

She took a step back, but he moved forward and caught her arm, stopping her. Reaching out, he brushed his knuckles gently across her cheek. "What are we doing?"

She huffed a shaky laugh. "Something we'll both likely regret."

The pad of his thumb grazed her lower lip, and need shuddered through her. "I don't want you to go," he murmured, his gaze never leaving hers.

Ava didn't reply. The sane thing to do would be to get out of this room right now. But her feet wouldn't move.

Fire quickened in her veins. Suddenly, she didn't care about anything except the fact that she'd die if he stopped touching her.

"We can keep it secret." She couldn't believe she was saying this, yet she couldn't stop herself. "No one will know."

He sucked in a deep breath, his broad chest heaving.

Ava's throat tightened. Suddenly, it was as if someone had just given her a hard slap. What the fuck was she doing? This wasn't just her own future she was playing with, but his.

She was going to be both *their* ruin.

"I shouldn't have said that, Jax," she muttered. "I'm not thinking straight. I'll go."

She stepped back from him and shifted toward the door. She needed to get out of here before her mouth ran away with her again.

However, he caught her by the shoulders, pulled her against him, and kissed her hard.

Ava groaned as his mouth savaged hers. Damn him, he tasted even better than she remembered. The heat of his body was a brand. Her hands slid up the hot skin of his naked chest as she kissed him back. Touching him like this made her palms tingle, made every nerve catch fire.

She wrapped herself around him, drinking him in.

A deep masculine groan rumbled through Jax's chest as he softened and deepened the kiss. His fingers raked through her hair, holding her head in place as his tongue thrust into her mouth.

His dominance turned her legs weak, and she sagged against him.

"Ava," Jax groaned against her mouth. "You drive me insane." With that, he reached down, grabbing fistfuls of her tunic and yanking it up.

Breathing hard, they broke apart, and she raised her arms so he could pull the tunic over her head.

Ava was naked underneath. She wore nothing but her amulet.

Jax shifted his attention to the droid charging on the opposite wall. "DT-45 ... shut down for three hours."

The droid gave an obedient bleep, whirring as it did as commanded.

Shivering with need, Ava stood there while Jax focused on her once more. His hot gaze raked over her. Likewise, she took him in, letting her attention drop to the massive erection tenting his pants.

She reached for it, letting her fingertips trace its hard, quivering length through the fabric.

Jax stepped close and placed his hands on her shoulders while she pushed down his pants. They slid to the floor, revealing the magnificence of his straining curved cock.

Ava's breathing hitched. A moment later, she lowered herself to her knees on the floor before him. He was as beautiful as one of the Gods, The Destroyer himself, and she'd worship him.

Her mouth hungrily closed around the hot tip of his shaft, and she drew him in as deep as she could, while her fingers closed around the thick base and gripped firmly.

A deep groan rumbled out of him. His fingers slid through her hair, cupping her head, urging her on.

Greedily, she sucked him, sliding her open mouth up and down his length and bringing him so deep she felt him hit the back of her throat.

Heat now pulsed between her thighs, a needy ache twisting low in her belly.

She'd wanted to do this on their first stolen night together, yet she hadn't summoned the nerve. But tonight, she shed her inhibitions. Who knew how this would all end, but she'd have her fill of him, she'd enjoy every inch of him, while she could.

She continued to suck him, her tongue flicking over his cock's swollen crown each time she withdrew. His heavy breathing and choked groans turned her frenzied, insatiable.

But with a whispered curse, Jax eventually pulled back.

His face was taut, his gaze burning as he stared down at her. "Keep doing that, Ava, and this will be over too fast."

Panting, she stared up at him, losing herself in the black depths of his eyes.

He reached for Ava then, hauling her to her feet. And then, it was him on his knees, sinking down before her. His mouth was on her breasts. He suckled her hard, almost to the edge of pain, while Ava gasped and writhed against him. However, after a short while, he ripped his mouth from her breasts and licked his way down between them.

And then he pushed her backward, walking her back to the wall.

Ava's spine hit cool, rough stone, yet she hardly noticed. All she could focus on was that he was now pushing her thighs apart. Taking hold of one leg, he slung it over his shoulder and turned her knee out, exposing her to him.

And then, when his mouth found her, his tongue delving and flicking with wicked precision, Ava bit down on her lower lip to stop herself from screaming. The wind was gusty outdoors, but there wasn't a hurricane raging around the temple tonight to obscure her cries. He might have shut down his droid overnight, but she had to be careful.

It was hard not to scream though, for he was now pleasuring her in a frenzy.

Ava gave a choked cry, her legs trembling. If he hadn't been holding her up against the wall, she'd have collapsed. She sagged against him as he pinned her there, devouring her.

A tide of pleasure broke between her thighs, rippling through her—and Ava shuddered, clapping a hand over her mouth to prevent herself from screaming. She bucked against him, riding the waves of pleasure.

But he wasn't done with her.

Jax pulled Ava down to the floor, flipping her over onto all fours. Legs and arms shaking, she braced herself as he slid into her.

This position was intense. She felt every curved, hard inch of him as he drove deep. And then, gripping her hips, Jax rode her in slow, measured thrusts.

Ava choked out a curse, angling herself up against him. He was big and filled her completely, yet she wanted more of him. She wanted *all* of him.

Each thrust was so powerful that she had to put out a hand onto the wall, to brace herself.

Heat and pleasure coiled deep inside, and she heard herself groan his name, begging for more.

Jax withdrew, flipped her onto her back, and thrust into Ava once more, bending one knee back so he could go deeper, harder.

The new position did it. He was hitting just the right place, deep inside, and she shattered in a storm of wet, throbbing heat.

Jax held himself over her, thrusting wildly now. And through her haze of pleasure, she watched him lose control. His face twisted, a nerve flickering in his cheek, and he threw his head back, his hoarse cry splitting the air as he came.

21. HUNTED

TWO KLICKS SOUTH of the temple, something crawled across the ground.

Moving like a spider over the rocky terrain, the droid scanned its surroundings. It had managed to avoid the patrol sweeping the area where it landed, although getting through the proximity beacons was harder.

It had been forced to disable one before moving ahead.

Soon, someone would notice the beacon was offline. But by then, it would be too late.

Metal fingers and toes dug into rocks as the droid inched forward. It was slow to travel this way, but necessary, for it was able to blend in with the ground and avoid detection.

The droid wasn't impatient. It didn't know what impatience was. Its entire focus was on the orders that had been programmed into it. Its mission. Time didn't matter—only success did.

Eventually, it crawled up the rocky hill behind the Temple of the Gods. The droid had deliberately skirted the back of the structure. It was easier to avoid detection. Armed guards were patrolling the pathway under the base, and one passed just above the droid.

Hanging there, as still as the rocks its dun-grey body blended against, the droid waited.

The thud of the guard's booted feet receded, and then the droid moved, crawling up to the path.

A moment later, it began to climb.

Jax stared down at Ava.

The look on his face made her breathing catch. She'd never seen that expression on him before—a mix of fierceness, pain, and longing that shot her straight through the heart.

It was the face of a man who'd had all his defenses stripped away.

Neither of them spoke.

They were both still panting in the aftermath of sex, both robbed of the words needed to respond to what they'd done.

Slowly, Jax withdrew from her, although the emptiness he left behind made her groan with frustration.

She still wanted more of him.

His mouth quirking, Jax shifted off her. But when he got to his feet, he scooped Ava up and carried her over to the bed. There, he lay her down before he stretched out beside her, propping himself up on an elbow so that he could look into her eyes.

"Regrets?" he asked softly.

Ava's throat constricted. "I should be sorry about this … but I'm not," she whispered. "I just wish we were different people … and that we'd chosen different lives."

His mouth curved once more, although his gaze was solemn. "We've made it hard for ourselves, haven't we?"

She nodded. "I won't give you up, Jax," she whispered. "Not unless I'm forced to."

His throat bobbed. "Let's hope it never comes to that."

"It won't … if we're careful."

He traced a lazy finger down her throat and into the deep valley between her breasts. Ava watched his long, blunt-tipped finger with its pale skin and black nail, remembering her reaction to him during their first meal together in the dining hall. She'd been equally intrigued, angered, and unnerved by this half-human, half-Vulkar warrior who'd just stormed into her life and tried to take control of it.

"I suppose that means I should send you back to your bed, Ava Mir-Brennan," he murmured. "Even though I'm not yet done with you."

The sensual promise in his voice, the way his hot palm now skimmed across her belly, made Ava gasp. "I can stay a little longer," she said breathlessly. "There's still time."

The droid climbed steadily using suction pads on its hands and feet, coiling its way around from the back of the temple toward the front.

Slowly, it worked its way up, and then it paused a moment, its golden gaze lifting to its destination. There, near the top, was a large window.

Plastered against the wall, it did a quick scan for threats.

Negative.

The time for caution had passed. It could move swiftly now, and it would.

The droid closed the remaining gap fast, rubber sucking on stone, and then grasped hold of the wide ledge, swinging up onto it with lithe ease.

It closed its right fist and smashed it through the windowpane. The window was double-glazed, yet the glass shattered under the powerful impact.

The sound exploded through the air, splintering the quiet.

Moving with precision, the droid unclipped something cylindrical from its abdomen and hurled it inside the bedchamber.

They were kissing, a slow, sensual exploration of each other's mouths, when the chamber shuddered.

Jax ripped his lips from Ava's, his body tensing as the stone walls continued to vibrate, a deep 'boom' reverberating through the temple.

Snarling a curse, he rolled off Ava and reached for his clothing, yanking on his body suit with swift, practiced ease.

"What was that?" Ava gasped. She too was now off the bed and dressing quickly. "An explosion?"

He nodded, strapping on his weapons. His gaze swept over her then, noting that she wasn't armed. Ava usually didn't go anywhere these days without a laser-blade strapped to her hip, and he wasn't about to let her do so now.

His heart started to kick against his ribs. Ava was in danger. He had to protect her.

"Here." He unclipped his own laser-blade and handed it to her. Jax still had his laser-pistol, which would have to do for now. "You need to get back to your quarters while the Guard deals with this. I'll escort you."

He expected an argument. Ava didn't submit to any orders without pushing back. But not now. Instead, she nodded, fastening the laser-blade around her waist. "Let's go."

Jax unholstered his laser-pistol and left his bedchamber, leading the way down the high vaulted corridor toward Ava's quarters.

However, when they rounded the corner that would take them to her door, Jax skidded to a halt, his gaze sweeping over the dust and smoke still billowing from the open doorway to the High Priestess's chamber.

"Fuck," he growled. His pulse started to thump in his ears, even as his senses sharpened.

Behind him, Ava gasped, yet he didn't take his gaze from the mess. "Draw your weapon and stay here," he ordered tersely. "I need to make sure the room is clear."

Without waiting for an answer, he moved forward, boots crunching on rubble, and approached the doorway.

The smoke was clearing, yet the acrid stench of burned circuitry and plastic caught at the back of his throat.

Halting in the doorway, Jax surveyed the damage.

It was a ruin. The ceiling had partially caved in, and the wall between the bedroom and the bathroom had been blown away. The windows were all punched out, and the High Priestess's droid lay on its side amongst the wreckage, a mass of fused metal.

Jax took a step back. It wasn't safe to go in, and he'd seen all he needed to anyway.

An instant later, claxons started blaring, echoing through the temple.

Jax moved back to where Ava waited for him.

"It looks to me as if a pyro-grenade went off in there," he informed her.

Ava's grey eyes widened further, her pulse fluttering in her throat. "DD-J3?"

He shook his head, giving Ava her answer.

Her face twisted, grief shadowing her eyes. He knew how much Dee Dee meant to her, but there wasn't any time to focus on it—not when someone had just tried to kill *her*.

His wrist-comm started vibrating then, and Jax answered it. "Vander. What's happening?"

"We have an intruder inside the temple, Sir," his Second's voice echoed through the hallway. "The sensors show it appears to have entered through the High Priestess's bedchamber. Is Lady Ava—?"

"She's safe," Jax cut him off. "I've got her. We're outside her bedchamber now. Where's the intruder?"

"Two corridors away, Sir. Wait … we've got a security-cam on it now." There was a pause on the other end before Vander muttered a curse.

"What?" Jax barked.

"It's a Hatchet-droid, Sir."

Jax's skin prickled. *Fuck.* He had to get her out of here.

"A what?" Ava asked, moving closer. Her face had paled.

"Something you don't want to ever meet," Jax replied, his blood roaring in his ears.

"It's moving toward you, Captain," Vander warned then. "In less than a minute, you'll have a visual. Get to the elevators now."

Jax didn't have to be warned twice. Gripping Ava by the arm, he steered her back the way they'd come. They then veered right, heading toward where a bank of three elevators glowed in the distance.

"Sir." Vander's voice boomed out once more. "It's coming up behind you … moving fast now."

Jax whipped around, pushing Ava behind him. "Call an elevator."

Meanwhile, he didn't take his gaze off the long corridor in front of him, where they'd just traveled.

Behind him, he heard Ava punch the call button with her fist. She then swore under her breath.

"What's wrong?" he demanded, not daring to look her way.

"It's dead."

"Try the others."

A pause followed, and then Jax spied movement at the end of the corridor. A second later, something tall and spindly, its metal carapace the same tawny hue as the surrounding walls, stalked toward them. Twin golden eyes fixed upon him, and cold sweat beaded on Jax's body.

Hatchet-droids were rare. They were a class up from the battle-droids the Mir-Ferrins used. These were slenderer, faster, and equipped with a reasoning capacity that was beyond most droids.

They were metal assassins, programmed to seek and destroy, and only the wealthiest members of society could have afforded one. And so, it seemed, could *The Creed of Truth*.

22. FACING THE ASSASSIN

JAX ACTIVATED HIS cyan-shield, and with a hiss, a translucent blue sphere erupted around him and Ava.

It wouldn't hold a hatchet-droid back for long, but it would buy them time.

Seeing his defensive move, the droid reached down with both hands, sliding free two laser-pistols from its legs.

Laser pinged through the elevator lobby, bouncing off the cyan-shield.

"They're all out." Ava's voice was brittle with panic. "The stairs are around the corner."

"There's no time to reach them," Jax ground out, holding the shield aloft as the droid bore down on them. "We'll have to fight it here." His gut clenched as he spoke these words.

He hadn't heard of any sentient fighting a hatchet-droid and living through the experience.

"Jax." Ava's hand grasped hard around his free arm. "I can't let you fight this thing … it's me it wants."

"Yeah, and it'll have to kill me first."

The grip on his arm tightened, her fingers digging through his body armor. "No."

"This is what I was hired for, Ava," he grunted. Sweat was trickling down his back as the hatchet-droid continued to fire upon them. It approached the lobby swiftly now, that predatory golden gaze never leaving them. "I swore to protect you … and I will."

Jax's gaze raked over the approaching droid, looking for a weakness, something he could exploit. This wouldn't be a fair fight. Once his shield went down, he was a dead man.

"Sir, backup is on its way." Vander's voice cut through the hum of the shield. "The elevators are all disabled, so we're taking the stairs."

Jax didn't bother to answer. They'd arrive too late to be over any help. Somehow, the droid had managed to drain the elevators of power. After destroying the High Priestess's bedchamber, and discovering that she wasn't there, it had located her on this floor and cut off the easiest escape route.

And now that she was just yards from it, the assassin was close to completing its mission.

Jax continued to examine the slender form that stalked toward him, its carapace gleaming in the soft downlights.

Halfway down its abdomen, his gaze halted.

The droid had a bandolier of pyro-grenades strapped across its front. As he'd suspected, it had used one of them in its first attempt to kill Ava.

An idea flowered then. It was a long shot, and he'd likely end up dead—but it might just save Ava's life.

"Ava," he barked, sweat pouring off him now. The cyan-shield was starting to spark and waver, a sign it was close to giving out. "I need you to wrench open the doors of one of the elevators. Do it manually, and then use your laser-blade to melt the lock so the door stays open."

"Right," she gasped, releasing his arm. "Onto it."

Jax wanted to help her, for the doors would take some force to open manually. However, he had to trust she was strong enough. He had to deal with this metal assassin bearing down on them.

He waited until the groan of metal behind him let him know that Ava was in the midst of completing the task.

"Okay," he growled as the hatchet-droid sheathed both its laser-pistols and reached for its laser-blade. "Let's go, motherfucker."

Jax dropped the shield and rolled, slamming into the droid, and carrying them both backward. And as they fell, he yanked a pyro-grenade from the bandolier.

Narrowly missing the burning heat of the ignited blade, he rolled off the droid and bounced to his feet, backing up.

A glance over his shoulder confirmed that Ava had opened the doors and melted the controls so they stayed open.

A second later, he did what every instinct in his body screamed against—what he'd told Ava he'd never do. He dived to one side, leaving her exposed to the hatchet-droid.

He was calculating on the fact that the assassin was after *her*. He was merely an obstacle in its path, and if he chose to remove himself rather than be exterminated, it didn't care. It was locked onto its target.

The hum of Ava's laser-blade igniting filled the lobby. Jax's heart kicked hard against his ribs. It was brave of her to try and fight it, but she wouldn't best a hatchet-droid in combat. She'd be cut down within seconds.

That gave Jax just a short window to act.

The hatchet-droid stood just a couple of feet from the yawning elevator shaft yet was oblivious to it.

Jax whipped behind the droid as it lifted its arms to strike Ava and slotted the pyro-grenade into the back of its utility belt. He then pulled the pin.

They now had ten seconds of grace before it detonated.

Not wasting time, Jax drove his shoulder into the metal assassin, ramming it with all his force.

The hatchet-droid staggered, and its strike went wide, scoring the wall next to Ava's head.

With a shout, she brought the glowing white blade of her weapon down, swiping hard against the droid's torso.

Metal sparked, yet the laser-blade didn't even score its armor.

Instead, it lifted its weapon again, recovering with frightening swiftness.

Jaw clenched, Jax backed up and then ran at the droid, slamming his left shoulder into it with such force that pain lanced down his side. Ignoring the agony, he sent the droid staggering into the breach.

An instant later, he caught hold of the edge of the shaft with his right hand, narrowly avoiding following the hatchet-droid into the void. Pain lanced down his left side once more, and he sagged to his knees.

The assassin tried to claw its way back, long legs and arms flailing.

Its long metal fingers caught around the edge of the floor, but Ava rushed forward, cutting down hard with her laser-blade, and sliced them off.

With a screech, the hatchet-droid fell.

Jax staggered to his feet and grabbed Ava with his right hand, for his left had gone numb, and yanked her away from the edge.

Two breathless seconds passed, and then the droid hit the bottom of the elevator shaft. A deep, resonant 'boom' thundered through the temple, shaking the floor on which they stood.

Breathing hard, Ava clung onto Jax, her arms entwined around his chest, as they both turned away from the billowing dust and debris that spewed from the open elevator shaft.

"I don't understand." Skylar's gaze roamed over Ava's face. Her Second gripped her hands hard. "How are you still alive?"

Ava hesitated. It was just for an instant, yet it was enough for understanding to light in Skylar's eyes. Her friend was sharp, and she'd already had her suspicions about Ava and Captain Jax.

"I wasn't in my bedchamber," she said, forcing herself not to avert her gaze. "I couldn't sleep, so I went to my solar to meditate … and was on my way back when the first explosion occurred."

Skylar nodded, although the disbelief in her eyes was evident.

Nonetheless, the other priestesses gathered around—eyes wide, faces ashen with shock that someone had dared send in an assassin to kill their leader—didn't have the same reaction.

"Thank the Gods," Sister Yinna whispered, her slender face pale with shock.

Her words caused a chorus of praise to ripple through the group. They all stood in the great chapel, before the altar. A ring of armored and helmed warriors surrounded them.

Ava forced a smile, even if her pulse was now racing. "I'm blessed indeed that they kept me safe," she replied.

Knowing she shouldn't, but unable to help herself, Ava glanced right at where Jax stood with his warriors. As always, he was a reassuring presence. A visor shielded his gaze, yet she could feel the weight of his stare as she'd briefed her priestesses on what had happened.

She'd never admit it to her sisters, but the Gods had little to do with why she was still alive.

Jax was the one they should all be thanking. His quick thinking and skill had saved her.

"Captain Jax," she said, trying to keep her voice composed. "Can you confirm the hatchet-droid has been destroyed?"

"Yes, My Lady," he replied. "The explosion blew it to pieces when it hit the bottom of the shaft."

Giddying relief fluttered through Ava, followed by a surge of adrenalin.

There had been no time for fear up there in the elevator lobby, but when she'd seen that droid striding toward her, its golden eyes spearing her like fiery darts, her bladder had tingled and her legs had turned to rubber.

Jax used the hatchet-droid's fixation on its target to his advantage. He'd moved fast enough to catch the assassin before it killed her.

It had been close though—and her breathing was still quick and shallow, her pulse fast at the memory of the cold, lethal laser skimming dangerously near her head.

Time had slowed down, and suddenly, all the things she took for granted—the steady beat of her heart, the strength in her limbs, the way her lungs inhaled and exhaled steadily—became more important than ever before.

Strangely, she'd never felt more alive.

She'd been scared, yet fear had sharpened her senses. When Jax needed her help, she'd acted. Her clear head had surprised her. What if she'd been in the wrong profession all these years?

In the aftermath, Ava's senses were still razor-sharp.

"Have you contacted the Wise Ones yet, My Lady?" Skylar asked. Her friend's gaze was shuttered now, and there was a coolness to her voice that had been absent earlier.

Ava's stomach bottomed out. Yes, Skylar knew.

Friendship didn't matter—their first loyalty was to this order and the Gods. How long would it be before her Second told the Wise Ones what the High Priestess had been up to?

Swallowing, Ava shook her head. "Not yet … I'll do that now. I just wanted to—"

Her wrist-comm started to vibrate then, a red light glowing upon the screen. Ava stared down at it, her pulse going wild.

It had been months, but finally, the Wise Ones were calling her.

Inhaling deeply, she raised her chin, her lips parting to say something. However, a loud buzzing to her right made her turn.

Her wrist-comm wasn't the only one vibrating this morning. Like hers, Captain Jax's wrist glowed red in the shadowy light inside the temple. It reflected off his armor, making him look as if he were covered in blood.

A wave of dizziness swept over Ava then, and it took all her effort to reach out and catch Skylar's arm to steady herself.

Why were they summoning the Captain of the Guardians too?

Only the High Priestess ever stood before the Wise Ones. It was unheard of for anyone else to set eyes on them.

Don't panic, she told herself as she deliberately avoided Skylar's eye now. Her Second would see her guilt written there, as bright as the beacon on her wrist. *Of course, they're hailing him too … the temple's just been attacked.*

Turning away from her sisters, Ava straightened her spine and faced Jax. "It seems the Wise Ones require a report in person," she said, forcing a calmness into her voice she didn't feel.

Jax nodded, his gaze still hidden from her by his visor. Yet the lower half of his face was stern. "Then we shall give them one, My Lady," he replied.

23. THE SUMMONS

THEY TOOK A special elevator up the Tower of Flame, one that Ava accessed via a retinal scan. The interior was mirrored, reflecting Ava's pale, strained face.

The face of a woman with secrets, a woman who'd broken her vows.

And worse still, a woman who intended to *keep* breaking her vows.

Jax had removed his helmet and carried it under one arm. However, unlike Ava, his expression bore no sign of guilt. Instead, he wore that same severe expression she'd seen on the day he arrived here.

The elevator jolted as it began its ascent from the temple, up the narrow, high tower, and Ava and Jax's gazes met upon the mirrored wall in front of them.

A second later, Jax's dark brows drew together, a crease forming between them. "Are you okay?" he asked softly.

"Not really," she whispered back. Truth was, she felt like throwing up—but she wasn't going to admit that to him.

They stared at each other for a moment, and then Jax moved close, his hand finding hers. He'd been wearing gloves earlier but had removed them just before they entered the elevator. She was grateful he had, for the feel of his fingers lacing hers, strong and warm, reassured her. "It'll be fine," he murmured. "They just want to be briefed on what happened."

Ava drew in a shaky breath. "But what if they *know*?"

His hand squeezed hers. "How could they?"

She gave a nervous laugh. "Maybe I'm just being paranoid."

Jax didn't reply. However, as the elevator continued its swift assent, carrying them high above the temple now, a muscle feathered in his strong jaw. "Whatever happens in there, Ava … I'm on your side," he said gruffly. "Just remember that, will you?"

Her chest constricted, her throat growing tight too now. Gods, there was so much she wanted to say to this man, but there wasn't time. "I will," she replied, her voice catching. "Thank you."

The elevator came to a shuddering halt, and Jax let go of her hand, moving away so that they stood an appropriate distance apart.

An instant later, the doors whispered open, revealing a plush lobby, decorated in red, silver, and black.

Two hulking battle-droids, their bronze carapaces gleaming in the overhead lights, waited for them, flanking a closed Lazda-steel door.

Ava's heart leaped at the sight of the droids. Just for a second, they reminded her of the hatchet-droid. However, these two menacing figures were gifts from the Mir-Ferrin clan-lord—insurance that no one could get into the tower and harm the Wise Ones. All the same, the sight of the laser-rifles slung over the droids' shoulders and the laser-pistols hanging at their sides put her even more on edge.

Both droids bowed their heads in deference as she approached, and Ava's pulse settled.

"Welcome, Lady Ava," one of them greeted her, its voice a low rasp. "The Wise Ones will see you and Captain Jax now."

Ava nodded to the battle-droids, plastering her most regal expression upon her face. She didn't look Jax's way, although she felt his presence, unwavering and unyielding, to her right.

The door whispered open, rolling back to reveal a rectangular gallery. Tall sandstone pillars lined an austere space while high tear-drop-shaped windows let in the pale red light.

Ava had only been up here once before—when the Wise Ones had sworn her in as High Priestess. She'd been waiting for their summons, for her predecessor had met them regularly, but none had come.

Not until today.

The Wise Ones looked over the Sisters of Awe, making all important decisions and ensuring the survival of the order. They were so old that they saw what other mortals didn't.

She started up the gallery, her boots whispering on the rough stone pavers beneath her feet, leading the way toward a raised dais.

Upon the platform sat two huge tempered-glass tanks, filled with pale-blue fluid and a maze of tubes and coils—and at the center of each floated folds of mottled purple flesh and a tangle of long sinuous limbs. Near the tanks, against the back wall, sat a row of utility-droids that serviced every need of the Wise Ones.

Behind her, Ava heard Jax's sharp inhale.

He would be surprised to discover the identity of the Wise Ones, as she had been the first time that she'd set eyes upon them. The High Priestess was forbidden to talk of the two beings residing in the tower, and no one else came up here, for only droids assisted them.

They were the last of a long-extinct race, as old as time itself. Ava had no idea what the race was, even though she'd tried researching them. Death might have come for the Wise Ones a long while ago too, if these tanks and the wall of twinkling lights, dials, and monitors didn't keep them alive. They'd seen empires rise and fall.

Ava broke into a cold sweat. Gods, she couldn't lie, not to *them*.

If they asked her whether she and the Captain of the Guardians of the Flame had formed an illicit attachment, she would have to speak the truth.

Bile stung the back of her throat. Suddenly, she wasn't ready. Not for this.

"Most revered ones," she greeted them, her voice carrying in the stone gallery. Ava then went down on her knees, bowing her head low. "I greet you."

She heard the scuff of boots and the scrape of armor as Jax followed suit. "Most revered ones," he said, copying her words. "I too greet you."

Silence followed, moments sliding by.

Ava's skin prickled. She had the feeling she was being watched, analyzed. Eventually, she glanced up, her gaze lifting to the dais once more.

The two beings inside the tanks hadn't moved, although now a row of small dark eyes had opened upon the top fold of flesh—and both the beings were studying them.

The silence continued, and Ava shifted uncomfortably. The cold, hard stone was starting to hurt her knees, and the Wise Ones' lack of response was unnerving. On the day they'd sworn her in, they'd both had plenty to say.

But not this morning.

Ava softly cleared her throat. "Most revered ones," she said, careful to keep her voice low and respectful. "Would you like me to brief you on the attack?"

"There is no need." A low, melodious voice echoed from an audio-pod at the front of the left tank. "We saw it all."

Sweat trickled down between Ava's shoulder blades. "But how?" she blurted without thinking. The Wise Ones didn't have access to the security-cams or the comms network throughout the temple. They were oracles, beings chosen by the Gods to preside over this order, but they had nothing to do with the day-to-day running of it. They'd always been reliant on the High Priestess to keep them updated.

Or so she'd thought.

"We don't need access to security-cams, Ava." A second, slightly lower voice vibrated out from the right audio-pod.

Ava's pulse went wild. It was as if the Wise One had read her mind. "You don't?" she asked weakly. The Gods strike her down, it was over. "But I thought—"

"Do you really think we'd allow ourselves to be isolated up here?" the second being asked, a slight note of rebuke creeping into its voice.

"And do you believe that we've existed for thousands of years without developing the ability to sense what is going on around us?" the first Wise One added. "We have ways of keeping ourselves updated."

Two rows of eyes fixed her now, and dizziness assailed Ava. She rocked back on her heels, placing a hand on the floor to steady herself.

Behind her, Jax was silent, but like her, he'd know what this revelation meant.

It was over—for them both.

"It was just as well you were absent from your chamber last night, Ava," the first of the Wise Ones continued, its voice gentling. "But that doesn't right a wrong."

Ava's tongue welded to the roof of her mouth.

"You took an oath when you joined this order," the second Wise One reminded her, unnecessarily. "But you have broken it … twice now."

Ava nodded. She wanted to look away, yet something—her battered pride maybe—made her hold firm. She'd done wrong, and she'd pay for it, but she'd not feel shame for what had happened between her and Jax.

Or for the way he made her truly feel alive.

"You have *both* broken the vows you swore," the first Wise One corrected its companion.

"What happens now?" Ava asked after a heavy pause. There seemed little point in apologizing. Surely, the Wise Ones didn't want her contrition? It was too late for that, and if they were all-seeing and all-knowing, as it appeared, they'd see into her heart and know she wasn't sorry.

Something twisted hard, deep inside her chest as the truth hit her.

Her only regrets were that she'd chosen a profession that she'd never been cut out for, and that the man she loved was about to be ripped from her.

She jolted at the realization. Yes, she should never have become a Sister of Awe. And yes, she loved Jax. Hopelessly. Desperately.

"These are trying times for the order," the second Wise One said, moving in its bath of translucent blue, its many folds rippling. "And we cannot afford to lose a High Priestess of your strength." It paused then, those dark eyes boring into her. "Captain Jax and his warriors were warned before their arrival that to have sexual liaisons with the High Priestess of Awe or any of her sisters is a crime punishable by execution" —Ava's breathing caught, as if someone had just punched her in the guts, yet the Wise One continued— "However, if you agree to undergo penance for your transgression, Captain Jax will be spared that fate. Instead, he will be sent to the salt mines of Cardashia, for ten years of hard labor."

Ava's heart started to kick against her ribs. "What?" she croaked.

"And what will Ava's 'penance' be?" Jax asked. Unlike Ava, he sounded surprisingly calm. Of course, he'd been expecting this. He'd known, all along, the price of touching her—known and not said anything.

But she'd had no idea. The Sisters of Awe had been cut off from the rest of the sector for so long, there was never any precedent for this. She'd believed he'd lose his job and end up being court-martialed—but not face execution or hard labor on a prison planet.

"The High Priestess will remain in solitary contemplation in the crypt under the temple," the second Wise One answered, those assessing eyes shifting behind Ava now. "There she will pray for forgiveness from the Gods … until they give her a sign."

"And how long will that take?" Jax asked, his voice cooling.

"It is not for us to say," the first being replied, his voice drifting down the gallery. "It could be one month … or six. That all depends on Lady Ava."

Silence followed these words.

Steeling herself, Ava glanced over her shoulder to where her lover knelt. His face was hard, although his eyes glinted. "Agree to it, Ava," he murmured.

They stared at each other for a long moment. It felt as if a weight were pressing down on her breastbone, making it hard to breathe. Heart pounding, she turned away from Jax and focused on the Wise Ones once more. "And what if I say 'no'?" she asked huskily.

"You will *both* be executed," the first Wise One replied, "Taken to the Sky Altar and sacrificed in the old way. The Gods will have their reckoning."

Ava's breathing stopped. It was far harsher than she'd ever imagined.

"Don't look so shocked, child," the first Wise One admonished her. "Did you not know that this was the punishment for breaking your vows?"

Ava shook her head, unable to speak. She hadn't. Her initiation rites hadn't mentioned it—they just demanded she make a vow of celibacy. After she and Jax had become intimate, she'd poured over the histories but hadn't discovered any such precedent. She'd read about High Priestesses being cast out of the order for bad behavior, but not executed.

The Wise One sighed. "It's been nearly two millennia since we've had to take such action. However, we wish to show you both mercy in this order's hour of need. Should you agree to show real penance, Captain Jax will live and you shall remain High Priestess of this order."

Hysteria bubbled up inside Ava. Mercy? Is that what they called it?

The Cardashian salt mines were a hostile place. As a child, her father had told her that those sent there barely lasted a year before the minerals in the salts poisoned them. Ten years wasn't life, but it didn't matter. It was a death sentence, all the same.

Something snapped then, a fragile cord inside her that had pulled tight over the past few months and been gradually fraying. It hit her then that none of this had any meaning anymore. Not the Wise Ones. Not even the Gods themselves.

Only the man standing behind her did.

"No," she whispered.

"Ava." Jax's voice behind her held a warning, yet she ignored him.

"No," she repeated, louder now. "I don't agree to this … to any of it."

24. DISPOSABLE

"THAT IS DISAPPOINTING, child," the first of the Wise Ones replied after a heavy pause. There was a sadness to its voice, regret even. "But if you won't repent, you will die."

Ava stared at the two beings floating in blue fluid in front of her. Like all her sisters, she'd always been in awe of the Wise Ones. To her, they'd always been benevolent beings—but no longer. She'd broken the rules, and now she'd pay.

"Ava, please," Jax said roughly. "You have a chance to save yourself ... take it."

Glancing over her shoulder, she met his gaze once more. "Would you prefer they sent you to Cardashia?"

His jaw bunched, and he shook his head. "I don't care what they do to me," he growled. "Only that *you* live."

"I won't let them send you there," she ground out. "Gasping for breath as your lungs collapse, your body riddled with weeping sores. At least both of us die with dignity."

They stared at each other for a few moments longer before Jax's gaze guttered and he favored her with a barely perceptible nod.

"So, that is your final word, Ava?" the second of the Wise Ones, the harsher of the two demanded.

"It is," she croaked, turning to face them again.

Gods, she felt sick.

"We didn't think you would reveal yourself as weak, child," the first Wise One said quietly. "Not like Keisha was. She wanted to step down from her role, to leave the order ... but we wouldn't permit it."

The queasiness within Ava grew, her mouth filling with saliva. Was that why Keisha had finally taken her own life? How alone she must have felt—especially when the Wise Ones showed her no compassion whatsoever.

"Take off the Amulet of the Gods … and lay it on the floor before you," the second Wise one commanded.

With trembling hands, Ava did as she was told. It felt strange to take off the amulet, warmed from her skin. After months of wearing it, the stone had become part of her. But at the same time, it was a relief. She was done here. Carefully, she placed it on the pavers. Its black surface winked back up at her, almost as if it were saying goodbye.

"Good … then there is nothing else to say." The being's voice took on a business-like tone. "Droids … take them down to the holding cells and prepare for the journey to the Sky Altar. And in the interim, send up Sister Skylar."

Ava's pulse started to thunder in her ears as she twisted around to see the two battle-droids move from their position against the door and approach down the gallery, their rubber-soled feet thumping against stone.

Heat swept over her, anger momentarily blotting out fear and grief.

Just like that, she was replaced. They didn't even bother to wait until she was out of the room before organizing her replacement.

She was disposable, and as easily forgotten as her predecessor, Keisha, had been. Rising to her feet, Ava realized she was shaking.

She met Jax's gaze once again as he stood up. His face was taut, his black eyes narrowed. There was a stillness she recognized in him, something dangerous and feral that writhed just beneath the surface.

She wondered if he was angry at her for sacrificing them both. She hoped he'd understood the reasons for her choice.

The battle-droids reached them then, each taking hold of a prisoner's arm and guiding them firmly toward the door.

Ava walked away without looking back at the two ancient beings who had just ordered their deaths. She realized now why the books she'd read said so little about the Wise Ones. It suited them to be shrouded in secrecy. The truth was they were feared as much as they were revered.

Walking side by side, so close their elbows touched, Ava and Jax left the gallery, crossed the lobby, and waited by the elevator.

The battle-droids stood with them silently.

The metal grip on Ava's arm was hard yet not cruel. She wouldn't easily break free though—and even if she managed to, where would she go?

The droids were taking them down to the holding cells that lay next to the crypt underneath the temple. The cells, designed for misbehaving priestesses, were never used—not until now.

The elevator doors opened, and the four of them stepped inside. It was cramped, and Ava and Jax were pushed together. The elevator plummeted, taking them back down into the temple.

Reaching out, Ava placed her free hand on Jax's chest. A thick layer of armor lay between them, preventing her from feeling the heat of his body. Shutting her eyes, Ava dug her fingernails into the gleaming surface of his breastplate. Gods, she couldn't believe this would likely be the last time she'd ever touch him. Desperation beat within her, fighting to get free. The sensation was so strong it hurt to breathe.

Wordlessly, Jax raised his hand and wrapped his fingers protectively around her wrist. He then squeezed.

She glanced up, and their gazes fused.

Jax stared down at her, his expression taut, fierce. "I love you, Ava," he said huskily. "Whatever goes down next, remember that."

Ava swallowed hard. "And I love you too," she gasped out the words. And she did. Her love for him was tearing her to pieces.

Something rippled across Jax's face—a blend of tenderness, grief, and determination. His lips parted, as if he was going to reply, but the jolt of the elevator and the hiss of the doors opening interrupted him. The journey up the tower had felt brief, but the return trip seemed over in an instant.

They'd run out of time.

Ava clutched at Jax's chest as the battle-droids towed them both out of the elevator, forcing them apart. They entered a small lobby, located behind the chapel, one that housed just this private elevator.

And then Jax moved.

She should have anticipated it, for there had been a warning of sorts in his words seconds earlier. But she hadn't—all she'd been focused on was that he loved her, and she loved him fiercely back—and she wasn't ready to give him up.

Jax was a formidable fighter, yet she'd never have expected him to take on two battle-droids, especially unarmed. They both left their weapons behind when they'd gone up to meet with the Wise Ones, and the droids were heavily armed.

A gasp escaped her as Jax threw himself up against the battle-droid gripping his right arm, drawing its weapon with his left.

Gods, he was fast.

Adrenaline ignited in Ava's veins. Yes. If they were dead anyway, they'd both go down fighting.

She slammed her elbow into the droid holding her, but the thing didn't budge. Jaw clenched, Ava twisted in its grip.

Meanwhile, Jax climbed the other droid like a ladder as it struggled to pry him loose. The battle-droid staggered, losing its balance, and the pair crashed to the floor.

The droid holding Ava drew its weapon and lifted it, leveling it at Jax.

No, you fucking don't! Using Jax's tactic, she drove herself against the battle-droid as it shot, and the bolt of laser went wide, leaving a deep, smoking score in the wall.

Another shot went off then, echoing through the lobby.

As they'd fallen, Jax had twisted around, raised the pistol to the back of the battle-droid's neck, and fired.

And the battle-droid had dropped like a stone, sprawling onto the paved floor.

Ava gasped, shocked that the droid had fallen so easily. However, its companion still had hold of her, and its grip on her arm was so hard now that her legs buckled under her. Sinking to her knees, she tried to pry its metal fingers loose, yet it was impossible.

Hissing a curse between clenched teeth, she let go of the hand and reached instead for the laser-blade strapped to the battle-droid's thigh.

Instantly, Jax was on his feet, and charging toward the remaining droid.

It fired again, but he was too close now; the fact that the droid was having to contend with a struggling human female allowed him to get under its guard. He threw himself at the battle-droid, knocking it backward.

But the droid righted itself quickly, coiled its free hand into a fist, and punched him hard in the stomach.

The blow was brutal, and even wearing armor, Ava heard the air rush out of Jax's lungs.

Igniting the laser-blade she now gripped, she drove it through the leg of her assailant. Sparks flew as metal melted and wiring sparked, and the battle-droid staggered.

"Slice into the back of its head," Jax wheezed as he struggled to get up from his knees. "It's a weak spot."

Ava pushed herself up from the floor, levering herself with her knees, and swung upward, bringing the blade down hard on the droid's metal shoulder.

The acrid odor of frying circuitry filled the lobby now, while the droid spun around, grasped her arms, and rammed her hard against the wall.

Ava's head cracked against stone, pain exploding in her skull.

For a moment, her vision speckled.

The battle-droid's grip was vicious, and she couldn't keep hold of the laser-blade. It deactivated and slipped from her nerveless fingers, clattering to the floor.

But her assailant had made a critical mistake.

In dealing with her, it had turned its back on Jax, just for a couple of seconds.

It was about to swing around again, bringing Ava with it, when another laser bolt detonated in the small lobby.

Suddenly, the punishing grip on Ava's arms released, and the droid crumpled. Its heavy metal skeleton sent a peel of thunder through the enclosed space.

Panting, while she rubbed her bruised arms, Ava's gaze met Jax's. He'd managed to stagger to his feet to take that shot. He was still half-bent over, and sweat covered his face.

"Jax!" Ava gasped. "Are you hurt?"

"Just bruised," he grunted. "And you?"

Her mouth quirked. "The same."

He flashed her a savage grin then. "Let's get out of here."

Shouldering one of the fallen droids' laser-rifles and handing a laser-pistol to Ava, he nodded to the exit. "We've got a minute at most before the alarms go off … this way."

Ava nodded, holstering the pistol. She didn't question him. It was clear Jax had a plan—he always did.

They left the lobby, moving through a corridor and into the chapel. As always, two sisters guarded the flame—two still figures in the shadowy light.

Ava glanced their way only briefly. She couldn't focus on the priestesses any longer. Her and Jax's lives hung in the balance now, and if they didn't get off this planet, they'd be dragged up to the Sky Altar and sacrificed.

And none of her sisters would prevent it.

Suddenly, all those within this temple, the priestesses, the warriors, and even the droids that had once served her, were no longer Ava's allies. As soon as word came down from the Tower of Flame, they'd turn on her.

She knew it with cold, dull certainty.

Until recently, she'd served this order faithfully. She was as devout as the rest of them in her beliefs—but now she'd crossed the line, that would cease to matter.

They traversed the wide floor, under the domed roof, past the rows of statues. The Galactic Gods and Goddess looked on in silence.

Leaving the chapel, Ava and Jax made their way through the long atrium toward the open doors to the temple.

As always, four of Jax's warriors stood guard there. Despite that they were covered in armor, their faces obscured by visors, Ava recognized them all—including Lieutenant Thresher, her sparring partner of late. The two women had become friends in the past month, but that was all done with now.

"Don't run," Jax whispered to Ava as they approached. "Not yet."

The warriors saluted their captain.

"How did it go upstairs, Sir?" One of them asked.

"As well as can be expected, Corporal Tate," Jax replied, his voice almost a drawl. "I will brief you all later."

He kept walking, Ava at his side.

"Sir?" Thresher enquired. Despite that Ava couldn't see her eyes, she marked the concern in the woman's voice. "Is everything all right?"

"It will be," he replied. "Remain at your posts."

They passed under the great stone arch and into the red-hued twilight.

Ava's gaze immediately swept to the landing platform, to where a shuttle sat. Her knees nearly buckled under her in relief. Of course, she knew Jax kept his shuttle out here most of the time; indeed, she'd seen it the evening before—but the sight of it, gleaming dull-grey in the weak sunlight, made her believe they might just escape.

They were halfway down the slope toward the landing platform when the alarms went off.

Claxons wailed, their shriek slicing through the air like a laser-blade.

Ava cursed, drawing her laser-pistol. The time for stealth was over.

The Wise Ones would surely know what had just happened, and even if they didn't, the claxons were loud enough to wake the dead. She wouldn't be surprised if the battlecruisers orbiting the planet could all hear them as well.

"Right," Jax grunted from next to her. "Time to run."

25. IN FLAMES

JAX SPRINTED DOWN the hill, waiting for the shouting to start behind him. It hadn't yet, but soon they'd come after him.

Ironically, despite everything that had happened, the Gods were on his side this morning. With Ava's help, he'd managed to best a hatchet-droid, of all things, before disabling two battle-droids. And his shuttle sat empty, waiting for him.

Often, tech-droids would be carrying out checks or maintenance on the craft, or some of his warriors would be onboard, readying it to go out on patrol.

But not now.

That didn't mean he could relax. Far from it. They weren't safe—and they wouldn't be until they were off-planet and hurtling through hyperspace.

Voices echoed down the hillside then.

Vander was shouting at him, telling him to halt, throw down his weapons, and give himself up.

Jax clenched his jaw and increased his pace.

Vander was a friend. They'd worked together for years. He could hear the strain in his first officer's voice; he was conflicted.

Hopefully, he wouldn't shoot Jax in the back.

It's over.

His career—everything he'd sweated blood to achieve over the years—was going up in flames before his eyes.

But Jax didn't care. All his life, he'd striven to make something of himself, to have a real voice in things. To lead rather than follow. But now it all seemed meaningless. The only thing he cared about now was Ava and getting her off this planet alive.

Laser bolts flew past then, scoring the ground. They were warning shots, close enough to let Jax and Ava know Vander meant business.

Jax cursed before grabbing Ava by the arm, pulling her close. He then punched his wrist-comm, activating the cyan-shield.

The blue sphere erupted around them, crackling as it settled.

Sweat trickled down Jax's back now as he ran. The last few yards to the shuttle, across the landing platform, suddenly seemed hundreds of klicks. Vander wasn't as conflicted as he'd thought.

A second later, a volley of laser hit the shield. It crackled, sending a shower of blue sparks overhead.

Jax's gut clenched. The cyan-shield had taken a hammering earlier in the morning from the hatchet-droid. It needed to be recharged and wouldn't protect them for long.

It didn't need to.

Tightening his hold on Ava's arm—for there was no way he was giving this woman up—he sprinted across the platform. Earlier, he'd guessed what was coming; he'd known what the punishment was for messing with the High Priestess of Awe.

He'd known, but that hadn't stopped him.

Slamming his hand on the panel next to the hatch, he waited while the shuttle IDed him.

Instants ticked by, and more laser crackled off the shield. The blue dome wavered and hummed, on the verge of going down. Ava pressed up against his side, her face taut as she glanced back the way they'd come. She gripped her laser-pistol at the ready, although she hadn't yet used the weapon.

Likewise, Jax hadn't unslung his laser rifle.

He didn't want to kill anyone. He just wanted to get off this planet.

Warriors poured out of the temple now, streaming down the hillside toward them. And at that moment, the cyan-shield failed, sputtering and dying with a spray of blue sparks.

"Fuck," Jax cursed. He needed the hatch to unlock. Now.

A metallic 'clunk' sounded, and with a hiss, the hatch started to lower.

Laser scored the fuselage, just a foot from Jax's head as he pushed Ava through the narrow gap and dived in after her.

Rolling to his feet, he slammed his hand down on the panel, closing the hatch. Jax sprinted forward, through the passageway and then the cabin, before launching himself into the cockpit and engaging the engines. Usually, he'd have gone through several preflight checks, but there was no time.

The shuttle shuddered, warning him that they were still firing on it.

And any moment now, someone would lob a pyro-grenade at them. If they did that with the shields down, it would blow a hole in the side of the shuttle, and they wouldn't be leaving.

That was why the first thing he did after engaging the engines was raise all shields, sliding them up to maximum.

The shuttle stopped shuddering.

Jax strapped himself in, glancing over at where Ava had just climbed into the copilot's seat. He was about to tell her to put on her safety harness, but there was no need. She was already fastening it.

Satisfied, he turned his attention back to the controls. "Hold on," he muttered. "This is going to be rough."

With that, he pulled back on the lever in front of him. The engines rose to a whine, and then the shuttle shot upward.

It was the fastest takeoff Jax had ever performed. It was a dangerous move too, for the G-force risked making the pilot black out. Indeed, a wave of dizziness swept over him as they rocketed into the sky.

Jaw clenched, he fought it, grasping onto the controls like grim death.

The shuttle bucked—no doubt hit by a pyro-grenade—but Jax paid it no mind. He was already using his free hand to chart a course on the nearest hyperspace lane. Once they cleared the planet's atmosphere, they'd have seconds before one of the battlecruisers locked on a tractor beam.

He had to make the jump fast.

Glancing sideways, Jax's heart jolted when he saw that Ava was slumped back in her seat, her head listing sideways. The takeoff had made her pass out. However, there was no time to try and revive her or to check she was okay.

He charted a course for the Leonis system. It was on the other side of Mir-Lelith territory, a lawless place that the clan-lord Aran Mir-Lelith did his best to pretend wasn't under his jurisdiction.

It was the perfect place to disappear.

Jax focused once more on the controls, sweat sliding down his back. Gods damn it, the nav-computer was taking an age to make the final calculations.

They were close to breaking free of the atmosphere now, the red curve of the planet stretching beneath them. To the right, Jax spied the crab-like shape of *The Star-Hawk*.

His ship.

It had been, but it wasn't any longer. He was a fugitive now—and Commander Asher was no longer his friend.

The light cruiser had maneuvered itself into position, and no doubt, Asher was getting ready to lock a tractor beam onto them.

"Come on," Jax muttered. "Finish up."

A green light blinked on the panel in front of him, signaling the final calculations had been made. The shuttle was ready to make the jump.

Jax just had to wait a couple more seconds.

And they were the tensest seconds of his life. The shuttle wouldn't make the jump while the planet's gravitational pull still held it. They had to be in the calm vortex of space.

His hand hovered over the controls, sweat pouring off him now.

The comm on the console in front of him started bleeping then, urgently.

Jax's mouth twisted. It seemed Asher was conflicted. He wanted answers before he arrested his former commanding officer.

There was no time for that, and Jax wouldn't be giving himself up.

Not in this lifetime.

However, Asher's hesitation bought him the time he needed. Jax slammed his fist down on the hyperspace panel.

The shuttle lurched forward, and an instant later, the red sphere of Pillarus One and the looming battlecruiser disappeared, replaced by distorted streams of silver light.

Breathing hard, Jax collapsed into his seat.

His heart still kicked against his ribs, although his limbs had gone weak.

There had been moments back there when he'd been sure they wouldn't make it. Yet they had.

He swiveled his chair right then, leaning forward to check on the woman slumped next to him. Reaching out, he cupped her cheek. "Ava?"

At his touch, she stirred, her lashes fluttering as she opened her eyes.

"What happened?" she asked groggily.

"The G-force during takeoff knocked you out," he replied. "You missed all the fun."

Her eyes widened, and she pushed herself up in her seat, glancing around. "Where are we?"

"In hyperspace, heading toward the Leonis system."

Her lips parted, and she swiveled back to him. "We made it?"

He grinned, even as his pulse still thudded in his ears. "Yeah ... we did."

"But how did you manage to make the jump without one of your battlecruisers firing on you?"

"I figured they'd try and lock a tractor on us rather than do that ... so I charted a course while we were making our ascent. Commander Asher tried to hail me, which bought us time. I made the jump the second we were clear of the planet's atmosphere."

Ava stared back at him, her grey eyes gleaming now. "I thought it was all over for us," she said huskily, shaking her head as if she couldn't believe this was real. "In the space of just a few hours, everything fell apart."

Jax's grin faded. "It did," he agreed. One minute they'd been lying in bed together, confident they could carry on their affair without anyone knowing, and the next, they were standing before the Wise Ones being condemned to death. It had passed in a nightmarish blur.

Ava's throat bobbed as she reached out, placing her hand on his arm. "You should have told me what the penalty was if you ever touched me."

"Why?" he asked quietly, his pulse quickening once more. "Would you have acted any differently?"

She swallowed once more. "Maybe."

A chill washed over Jax. "Are you sorry we did this?"

Her gaze widened, even as she shook her head. Her grip on his arm tightened. "Never," she said, her voice roughening. "But it would have tempered my recklessness if I'd known your life was at risk."

Their gazes fused, silence filling the cockpit, broken only by the throb of the engines.

Jax's chest constricted, his heart racing now as he raised his hand and cupped her cheek. "I passed the point of no return a long time ago, sweetheart," he murmured. "But I only realized it today."

Her eyes widened at his admission, her chest rising and falling.

"You freed me, Ava Mir-Brennan ... I never knew what was missing in my life until we met" —he broke off, fierce emotion clutching at his chest— "And I'll die before I let anyone hurt you."

She offered him a tremulous smile before murmuring, "You've shown me who I really am, Jax. It seems we're *both* free now."

Drawing back, Jax unclipped his safety belt. He then released her restraints and pulled Ava close so she was perching on his lap.

She nestled against him with a sigh, their bodies curving together perfectly. "What now?" she asked, her lips tracing the column of his neck.

He sighed. The feel of her mouth against his skin made all the tension, all the adrenaline, of the past few hours drain from him. Ava had a way of making him forget everything but her. "Now ... I guess we work on disappearing ... for good," he replied distractedly.

Ava raised her head, meeting his eye. "But what if I don't want to?"

Jax inclined his head. "What?"

"I can't forget that meeting we had with the clan leaders ... everything you said about the need to actively go after *The Creed of Truth*. Go on the offensive rather than the defensive."

He cocked an eyebrow. "Yeah, I said that," he admitted. "But that was before it all turned to shit." He paused then, noting the serious look on her face, the glint in those grey eyes. "Do you really still care ... after everything that's happened?"

Ava surprised him by nodding, her jaw firming. "I do."

"Why?"

"Because whether or not I'm part of the Sisters of Awe, I don't want *The Creed's* influence to grow. I still care about what happens to the order ... and about this sector and those who reside within it ... as do you."

He stared up at Ava, considering her words. She was right. He did.

Her mouth lifted at the corners then. "Besides, you'll get bored just sitting around, hoping the authorities never find you … as will I." She paused, her smile widening. "Come on … you know you want to."

Jax answered her smile with one of his own. He reached up then to glide the pad of his thumb along the sensual swell of her lower lip. "All right," he murmured.

EPILOGUE. HUNTING THE CREED

A year and a half later …

CROUCHED IN THE dark, cold tunnel underneath the city, Ava wondered if she was losing her mind.

If someone had once told her she'd be crawling around under Ard, Caldoros's capital, searching for the hidden entrance to a terrorist lair, she'd have laughed it off as crazy talk.

Yet here she was, wearing kneepads and gloves, with a headlamp strapped on, exploring the passages that led under a large building that flanked the city's central plaza.

She'd charted the network of metal tunnels, set into the bedrock here, that ran under The Bank of Caldoros, a massive building that took up an entire block. These passages weren't made for humans, but for wheeled droids that transported goods around what would be the basement level of the building to the various service elevators. It was a real warren, but Ava carried a nav-monitor strapped to her arm. She wouldn't get lost.

Crawling fast, she was grateful for the knee-guards on the unforgiving metal. It was Yedlas, a national holiday that heralded the end of summer, so the building above her was empty, and as such, there were no deliveries scheduled. She'd checked. She wouldn't run into any droids or set off intruder alarms.

On and on, she crawled, charting each passage she passed through, while she looked for anything that would lead her down below the service tunnels.

If she couldn't find it, this trip would have been a waste of time—and disaster might strike.

Desperation was starting to claw at her when she turned the corner of a tunnel and spotted a metal hatch straight ahead.

It was rusted shut, and she had to use a spray from her utility belt to loosen the lock, but she finally managed to unscrew it. Then she drew the hatch open and slid down into the tunnel below, climbing down a ladder.

Ava realized then that she'd entered a disused ventilation shaft. Spiderwebs festooned the walls, looping like washing lines through the tunnel. They clung to Ava's clothing as she descended. Clearly, no one had climbed down here in a long while.

Reaching the bottom of the ladder, she moved carefully now, quietly, wary of making any noise. If this was leading her to where *The Creed* was hiding—and she hoped it was—she had to be careful. Ava switched off her headlamp and dropped to her hands and knees once more, moving over to a large wire mesh, where light filtered up.

Even before she reached it, she could hear voices.

Ava's pulse quickened. The information they'd managed to get hold of a week earlier wasn't false, after all. Those bastards had dug a tunnel under this city, directly under the central plaza. It had taken them years, a project of great stealth, yet they'd finally achieved it.

Thank the Gods, she and Jax had decided to check it out.

Reaching the edge of the grate, Ava looked down.

Robed figures moved around approximately eight feet below her. They stood in a cavern of sorts, as if their tunnel had found a natural opening in the rock. Nearby, she could hear the trickle of running water.

Ava grinned. She'd found them, all right.

Most of those below her appeared human, or they did from this angle, and they all had shaven heads—a mark of those who followed Wis. However, it was hard to tell devotee from fanatic these days. They all wore black and spoke to each other in low, somber voices.

Ava squinted, trying to make out through the play of light and shadow what they were doing.

Moments passed, and then she caught sight of the dull-grey metal boxes they carried. They all seemed to be traveling in the same direction.

"These are the last of them," one male muttered. "Thank Wis."

"Yeah," his companion replied. "There'll be enough pyro in that stack to blow half this city to kingdom come when it goes off."

"But it'll be the clan-lord who gets roasted first," someone else quipped. "That's all that matters."

Around them, laughter echoed through the tunnel before someone hissed, "Quiet … or Father Cillan will have our balls."

The laughter abruptly cut off, and the acolytes continued in silence.

Heart pounding now, Ava drew back, logging the coordinates from her nav-monitor onto her wrist-comm. She'd heard enough. If she lingered much longer, she risked accidentally making a noise and alerting them to the fact they had an eavesdropper.

She had everything she needed—it was time to go.

Her trip out of the warren of dark metal passageways seemed to take an age. All the while, the nav-monitor bleeped and whispered to her, guiding her through the maze.

As she crawled, Ava was aware of the passing of time.

Jax would be waiting for her call, and soon the clan-lord himself would descend from his fortress carved into the mountain above the city to give his Yedlas speech.

She had to get out of these metal tunnels so she could connect to the Sectornet.

Eventually, dripping with sweat and gasping for breath, she pushed her way out into the dark passageway at the back of the building. Even here, she could hear laughter and singing from the thick crowds of revelers who'd be making their way into the central plaza.

Dropping down on her backside, she didn't bother to replace the hatch. She'd do that afterward. Instead, she punched her wrist-comm with her finger and opened a channel to her lover.

Jax answered immediately. "Ava."

"I found them," she gasped, swiping her comm screen. "I'm sending you the coordinates now."

"It's true then?"

"Yeah … they've dug their way into an underground cavern of some sort, and they're loading it up with pyro-detonators. When it goes up, it's going to destroy half the city." She broke off then before adding. "And they mentioned Father Cillan."

A pause followed before Jax replied, "Why am I not surprised that asshole is behind this?"

In the months they'd been hunting *The Creed*, they'd discovered that one of the most active terrorist cells was led by a human male named Father Cillan.

"When?" Jax asked then.

"They're timing it with the clan-lord's speech."

"Great." His tone was grim. "We've got to move then."

"Where are you?"

"A block away."

"I'll meet you later." Ava paused, knowing that they couldn't linger over this conversation, but unwilling to cut the call, nonetheless. "Jax."

"Yes."

She swallowed, fear tightening her throat. This was what they'd been working toward ever since fleeing Pillarus One, but suddenly, she was afraid. She'd taken risks this afternoon, but the part she'd played seemed easy compared to what he had to do now. "Be careful."

"Don't worry," he replied, his voice softening. "I will be."

Ava waited for Jax in their agreed meeting place, upon a ridge high above the city—a spot that had an unobstructed view over the skyline. However, Ard's central business district was packed with tall buildings, so she couldn't see the central plaza from here.

It was a tense wait, and it was hard not to start pacing—not that there was space for that, especially if she didn't want to fall to her death.

Ava had only just completed the climb up to the ridge, and was recovering her breath, when the sirens began, their wail echoing over the city and across the mountainside.

Sirens were good. It meant that Jax and his team had managed to alert the authorities. But when the laser fire started and smoke began drifting up from between the tall buildings, Ava's stomach began tying itself in knots.

Was Jax involved in that?

He and his team were supposed to get in, deal with the terrorists, and then get out before alerting the authorities.

Had something gone wrong?

Time drew out, and Ava started biting her nails. She wasn't a nail-biter in general, but her nerves were getting to her. Night fell, and a single golden moon rose into the deep-purple sky. But still, there was no sign of Jax or the others.

Ava started to feel sick.

Hunting *The Creed* had been her idea, although Jax made it clear he was as dedicated as she was to bringing them down. But right now, she was terrified she'd lost him.

And without him, nothing would matter anymore.

The past year and a half had shown them both what love was. Jax was tough and brutal, but with her, he was tender and loving. She saw the private side to him, the side he'd long learned to hide from others.

Jax was the missing part of her soul she'd waited all her life to find.

"Damn it," she muttered, glancing down at her wrist-comm for what felt like the hundredth time in the past ten minutes. "Where are you, Jax?"

"You called, My Lady?"

A familiar voice rumbled in her ear, and Ava whipped around only to be crushed against a broad, hard chest.

"Thank the Gods," she gasped, squeezing him in a hard hug. "I was beginning to panic." Ava drew back then, peering around him at the shadowy figures, all wearing dark cloaks, making their way down to the edge of the ridge, between the trees. "Did you lose anyone?"

"No," Jax replied, and her knees went weak with relief.

Ava turned then, leaning against his strength as she gestured to where smoke still curled up from the city below and sirens wailed. "What happened down there?"

"We got into the tunnels through the coordinates you sent and found the cache of pyro-detonators, all waiting to go off. We killed those guarding them and fused the timers. We then brought down the exit tunnel, cutting off access to those waiting beyond, and escaped using your route." He paused, his arms wrapping around her. "However, when we got outside, we heard there had been an attack on the central plaza. Father Cillan led the surviving members of his unit. They stormed the plaza just as the clan-lord was about to give his speech."

Ava tensed. "But that's a suicide run."

"Yeah, it was a real mess down there … that's why it took us so long to get out. They've locked the city down."

"And the clan-lord?"

"He's fine." There was no missing the edge to Jax's voice. He was a Mir-Lelith, but his one meeting with his clan-leader had left a sour taste in his mouth. "Scurried back up the mountain to his lair as soon as he caught a whiff of trouble."

Ava's gaze traveled over the smoking city. "It's done then," she murmured.

"It is. This cell has been dealt with … but there are others." Jax's voice sharpened then. "And we'll bring them down … one by one."

Ava turned in the circle of his arms, raising her chin to meet his gaze. "We will," she vowed with the same vehemence. She then lifted a hand to caress his strong jaw. "But tonight, just enjoy this victory … you've worked hard enough for it."

And he had. They both had. With no funds and no backing from the clan leaders, it had taken a while to amass a team of fighters with the skills and the dedication to take on *The Creed*—yet they'd succeeded.

Finally, they were living the life they both wanted; one where they only answered to each other, no one else. They were truly free.

Jax stared down at her, his face all hollows and planes in the golden moonlight. "You also did well tonight," he murmured. "I was worried you wouldn't find a way in … but you did."

She smiled back, warmth suffusing her chest. His praise meant a lot to her. "I wasn't going to fail," she replied. "Everything was riding on me finding it."

"You're a force of nature, Ava." His lips brushed the shell of her ear while his hands slid down her back possessively. "I shouldn't have doubted you."

Ava sighed, melting into him as his mouth found hers. His kiss was deep and sensual. He didn't care that the rest of their team now stood around them. The others were too intent on watching the unfolding drama below to pay attention to Jax and Ava anyway.

When Ava drew back from the kiss, she was breathless and weak. "Gods, I love you," she whispered.

She *was* tough, but then Jax Mir-Lelith needed a partner strong enough to handle him. She wouldn't let anyone, or anything, stand between them. They'd been hunted ever since their escape from Pillarus One, yet they always managed to be one step ahead of the special forces the clan leaders had sent after them.

No one would realize what they'd done tonight. No one would take the price off their heads. It was a thankless task, but Ava didn't care. They hadn't done this for the gratitude of the clan leaders.

They'd done this because it was necessary.

"So, you love me, do you?" Jax's tone was teasing as he leaned down and brushed his lips over hers once more.

"Arrogant asshole," she whispered back. "You're supposed to tell me that you love me too … that you'd cross the universe for me."

Jax's mouth quirked, in that sexy way that made her heart stutter. "Oh, I do, Ava … and I would," he assured her, taking hold of her hand. He then drew her away from the edge of the ridge, back toward the privacy of the pines carpeting the mountainside behind them. "But talk is cheap. Come with me, sweetheart, and I'll show you."

The End

GALACTIC CLAN WARS GLOSSARY

The three dominant clans of the Rith Sector

Mir-Brennan
Clan insignia: a shooting star above a clenched fist.
Clan motto: Glory is the reward of valor
Clan color: gold

Mir-Ferrin
Clan insignia: crescent moon and twin crossed blades
Clan motto: Righteous and devoted
Clan color: bronze

Mir-Lelith
Clan insignia: a silver full moon with a shooting star
above it
Clan motto: We do not forget
Clan color: silver

Galactic gods

Jidea: Goddess of Fortune
Wis: the Seer of Truth
Aura: Goddess of Prosperity
Fara: Goddess of Light
Nain: Goddess of Darkness
Syr: God of Mercy
Raul the Destroyer: God of War
Miradia: Goddess of Fertility.
Examples of lesser deities: Bron the Worthy/Eldra the
Wise

Technology and Weapons:
A pyro-grenade/detonator/pyro-torpedo: heat incendiary
devices
Ardex: latex-style material
cyan-shield: a glowing blue sphere that is triggered from
a device strapped to the wrist
Klick: a term used to denote one kilometer or 1,000
meters

Laser-blade: a futuristic sword or dagger that consists of a grip with three settings. Blue is practice/spar, orange is stun, and white is kill

Laser-pistol or rifle: Energy output for practice is zero, fifty percent for stun, and anything over eighty percent is lethal

Lazda Steel: highly durable metal

PCSD: a small Portable Currency Storage Device, which contains hard credits

Public Sectornet: a comms network publicly available throughout the sector

Shadownet: a comms network used by the criminal underworld

Wrist-comm: a small communication device worn on the wrist

Different classes of droids
Battle-droids
Utility-droids
Server-droids
Ticketing-droids
Hatchet-droids

ABOUT THE AUTHOR

Samantha Charlton is a multi-award-winning-author of Amazon best-selling Historical Romances, writing under a nom de plume. However, she doesn't just have a passion for the past, but also the future. She fell in love with Han Solo at an early age and began a lifelong love of Sci-Fi adventure and Space Opera. This led her to writing Space Opera—with emotional and steamy romance—of her own!

Connect with Samantha online:
www.samanthacharltonauthor.com
www.facebook.com/samanthacharltonauthor
Email: samanthajcharlton@gmail.com